RISING

by

FENEK SOLÈRE

Counter-Currents Publishing Ltd.
San Francisco
2017

Cover design by Kevin Slaughter

Cover Image: Yevgeny Vuchetich, *The Motherland Calls*,
Volgograd, Russia

Adapted from
https://www.flickr.com/photos/jakuza/6111636957/
under Creative Commons License

Published in the United States by
COUNTER-CURRENTS PUBLISHING LTD.
P.O. Box 22638
San Francisco, CA 94122
USA
http://www.counter-currents.com/

Hardcover ISBN: 978-1-940933-29-0
Paperback ISBN: 978-1-940933-30-6
E-book ISBN: 978-1-940933-31-3

Library of Congress Cataloging-in-Publication Data

Names: Solère, Fenek, 1972-author.
Title: Rising / by Fenek Solère.
Description: San Francisco : Counter-Currents Publishing Ltd.,
[2016]
Identifiers: LCCN 2016008873 (print) | LCCN 2016020765
(ebook) | ISBN 9781940933290 (hardcover : alk. paper) | ISBN
9781940933306 (pbk. : alk. paper) | ISBN 9781940933313 (e-
book) | ISBN 9781940933313 (E-book)
Subjects: LCSH: British--Russia (Federation)--Fiction. | Politi-
cal fiction.
Classification: LCC PS3619.O43253 R57 2016 (print) | LCC
PS3619.O43253 (ebook) | DDC 813/.6--dc23
LC record available at https://lccn.loc.gov/2016008873

To EM—
for the good times and the bad,
for they were always memorable

1.

'Seatbelts, please', announced the pilot as BA879N smashed through a plate glass sky. 'We'll be landing at Pulkovo in five minutes.' Professor Tom Hunter felt a rush of anticipation as the plane glided over the Gulf of Finland, cutting across Krasnoe Selo, bearing down on a city that Hitler once decided 'to level, make uninhabitable, and relieve us of the necessity of having to feed the population through the winter.'

From his window seat, the much-maligned Thomas Hunter, PhD of London squinted at a chequerboard of flooded fields through electrostatic twilight. A vast empty land, the Ulyanka, slashed by railway lines, stretched tight and taught like bowstrings ready to fire. Highways edged by gas pipes, tall residential blocks, and belching chimney stacks tarnished a beautiful Baltic sunset. Sitting targets, he surmised, for the militant sects now harassing the Motherland.

Ears popped as the 747 went into freefall, wings wafting down through air pockets, drifting on water vapour, wheels locking in place with the gratifying grind of hydraulics. Reports of the Great Migration and the Third Chechen War were still fresh in his mind as the lights of the control tower came into view. They hung like a necklace of septic pustules around the tattered Federation flag, luminous orange circles intersected by the insect silhouettes of ground staff running back and forth, shadow people from an Orwellian novel.

When tyres hit tarmac, the sudden sparking jolt tested his seatbelt. Half-hearted applause rang out. The superstitious Slavs thanked God and the flight-deck for a safe landing. A voice crackled over the intercom, asking restless passengers to remain seated until the ground crew were in position. Predictably, everyone ignored the advice, scrambling for hand luggage, throwing open overhead lockers, blocking the aisle with bulky hips and bulging bags of duty free. The ping of SMS messages sang in breast pockets.

Claustrophobic moments followed, then the doors opened, allowing a ghostly mist to enter the dimly-lit cabin. People shuffled forward, disembarking onto the docked platform. When the Professor descended the rattling steps, a strong gust caught his flapping coat, black moleskin billowing, until he gathered it in and buttoned it under his chin. Tom surveyed the burnt ochre skyline as he crossed the runway's metalled surface. The airport had suffered rocket attacks by insurgents. Walls were pockmarked from small-arms fire. News of the almost daily terror attacks on Russian civilians angered him. Muslim militia roaming along the banks of the Kamenka River near Suzdal had nailed a ten-year-old virgin, cruciform style, to the golden door of the Cathedral of the Nativity. Rumours that the Tartar population of Sviyazhsk in Ingushetia were drowning Whites in the Kuybyshev reservoir had now been verified by independent sources.

His eyes cruised over the news channels on his handheld:

- ❖ The American President is assassinated when his motorcade comes under sustained attack from an armed resistance group in Denver, Colorado;
- ❖ Mass riots continue across the United States with hundreds dying in shootouts in ethnically mixed cities from New Orleans to Baltimore;
- ❖ A state of emergency is declared and Chicago Mayor Rahm Emanuel is nominated to lead a coalition government in an attempt to unite citizens behind the New America Foundation;
- ❖ Russian ground assets deployed around Hama and Homs are over-run by American-backed Syrian rebels supported by Wahhabist forces using TOW

anti-tank weapons, firing air-to-ground missiles at low flying Sukhoi SU-30's operating over Latakia;

❖ Israeli forces clash with Russian army contingents around Tel al-Harah in the Golan Heights;

❖ George Soros addresses a NATO-led summit in Bucharest involving leaders from the Baltic and Central European states, including Lithuania's President Dalia Grybauskaitė, Latvia's Raimonds Vējonis, Hungary's Janos Áder, and Poland's Andrzej Duda, insisting that Russia ceases its aggressive and expansionist behaviour or face the threat of military confrontation;

❖ The evacuation of Russian military forces from the Bassel al-Assad airbase in Syria coincides with Israeli airstrikes on the Bushehr nuclear power plant in Iran;

❖ The EU enforces oil sanctions, and the Swedish-based Preem company, owned by Mohammed H Al-Amoudi and Poland's PKN Orlen refineries begin purchasing cheap Saudi crude oil;

❖ President Putin faces a vote of no confidence in the State Duma and is impeached. The Chairman of the Russian Central Bank is placed under arrest;

❖ A snap election returns the Eurasian Party to power, but the government soon fractures along ethnic lines, with the Asian wing joining the *Coalition for Renewal* led by Issur Babel;

❖ A further election results in President Babel's *Coalition* movement winning office and the new incumbent taking up residence in Ryad 1, before submitting the following nominations to lead the Federation Council , the Upper House of Parliament, the Constitutional Court, the Supreme Arbitration Court and the post of Prosecutor General of Russia, respectively: Mendel Abelev, Boris Abras, Grinda Azel, Raisa Feldman, and Isak Shapiro;

❖ Alexander Dugin evades arrest and is safe-housed by the emerging European Resistance in Prague;

- ❖ Federal compensation for wrongful prosecution are considered for a range of individuals, including Leonid Nevzlin, Mikhail Khodorkovsky, Vladimir Duvdov, and Michail Brodno, all of whom were involved in the Yukos scandal and, with the exception of Khodorkovsky, were thought to be residing in Israel;
- ❖ President Babel's first legislative act is to pass an edict to suspend the State Duma pending its support for his more liberal approach to foreign policy, internal security, and immigration;
- ❖ Yeltsin family members publicly endorse President Babel's reforms from the steps of their Gorki 9 residence;
- ❖ Putin is held under house arrest at Novo-Ogaryovo;
- ❖ The Pyotr Velikiy battle cruiser is scuppered in Sadya Bay;
- ❖ Two new Borei-class SSBN submarines undergoing sea trials near Spitsbergen are surrendered to a NATO flotilla operating out of Bodo.

He felt the wind pull at his hair, eyes registering the cityscape, witnessing scenes reminiscent of Dmitry Glukhovsky's futuristic fiction *Metro 2033*. A stewardess appeared like a genie smothered in smog, blue scarf whipping in a rotor's tail-wind. She was pointing to a ramshackle bus, something the Wehrmacht might have deserted at the end of their nine-hundred-day siege. Insects dotted a mud-splattered chassis. A militia man with a GSh-18 automatic waved the passengers on, climbing aboard, reaching for the leather straps dangling like NKVD ropes from the stained roof. With a clunky churn the engine ground into gear, dragging the potbellied pig one hundred metres across the runway. Gasping and choking, steam spraying from a perforated radiator, the lumbering beast came to a hissing halt just short of the gulag-grey terminal.

Carried by the momentum of the crowd through the

arrivals lounge, the dissident academic waited in line behind nursing mothers, snub-nosed businessmen, and self-
conscious tourists, his mind computing second thoughts
about having made the trip. Flat screens showed live images of a bombing in Ufa, a city in the distant Ural Mountains: eviscerated skin threading bloody snow. It seemed
the Wahhabist-inspired International Army of the Mujahideen were claiming responsibility for the attack which
had killed thirteen people and injured a further twenty
four at a supermarket complex in the Tsyurupy district. Dr
Hunter knew the city to be a key industrial and transport
hub on the confluence of the Ufa and Belaya rivers. A
prime location for rebel Bashkirs to cut the Trans-Siberia
railway line and the M5 Ural and M7 Volga motorways.
Obsessively checking the entry dates etched into his visa,
he rode the escalator towards passport control. His mind
focussed on the conference he was due to speak at, only
too aware that his arrival may not be welcomed by certain
political circles, particularly after the recent elections and
the demonstrations that followed the plebiscites. Initially,
voters had returned the more nationalist Eurasian Party to
power in the State Duma, but within weeks the ideological
split between the Rus- and Turkic-centric wings had rendered it dysfunctional. Alexander Dugin became a scape-
goat, with the majority of political commentators arguing
that 'realpolitik' demanded the new President's acquies-
cence to the realities of the international situation:

❖ The signing of the Gdansk Charter by which Russia
  agreed to find a political rather than a military response to what was now being termed 'the Great
  Migration' of Chinese, Turkic, and Muslim peoples
  into its living space;
❖ The EU and the US deploy missile systems in Poland and the Czech Republic in advance of sending
  peacekeeping forces into Western Ukraine;
❖ The Russian Duma introduces a third wave of
  sweeping austerity measures as a result of the on-

going financial crisis that had begun in 2014;

❖ An analysis estimates that two-thirds of Russians live on the poverty line; every winter they die off in their thousands as the temperatures drop outside their crumbling apartment blocks;

❖ $300m wiped off investments in a single 24-hour period and a 30 percent depreciation of the rouble against a basket of currencies.

Social disintegration seemed inevitable as wave upon wave of immigrants overwhelmed cities, towns, and local communities between Vorkuta and Saratov. Compounding this there was continuing evidence that the European Union, the US government, and various NGOs were still pouring money into so-called democratic groups to further destabilise the country. Adding insult to injury, Pussy Riot's Nadezhda Tolokonnikova and Maria Alyokhina had been awarded the Nobel Prize for Literature. This was followed rapidly by worldwide coverage of the publication of Mikhail Khodorkovsky's proposed new constitution for Russia and his tumultuous reception at Ben Gurion airport, where he was welcomed with open arms by the leader of the Knesset.

Despite recent outrages against native Russians in South Ossetia and Grozny, it was clear that the anti-Russian narrative in the Western press, starting with the sabre-rattling after the downing of a Malaysian passenger flight over Torez, was not going to slacken. Alleged atrocities by the 108th and 5th Motor Rifle Divisions and the 860th Separate Motor Rifle Regiment in Surgut and Salekhard were being investigated by Commissioners from the UN's War Crimes Tribunal. Media frenzy followed the retaliatory cluster bombing by Russian SU-24 fighters against *bandformirovaniya*, literally bandit formations, roaming the countryside ethnically cleansing the land of Whites to create new Muslim settlements in Dombaj, Sukhumi, and Elista. Further accusations of human rights abuses from Magadan in the east to Tver in the west were broadcast on

CNN, the BBC, and Al Jazeera. The signs were ominous: Parnas, the liberal grouping, and larger-than-life characters like Navalny, Dobrokhotov, and Kozlovsky were being portrayed as heroes. Chechen warlords like Aslan Maskhadov, Abdul Halim Sadulayev, and Dokka Umarov were spoken of in reverential terms. The Russian GDP had fallen for the seventh year in succession and OPEC continued to pump the market with petroleum, keeping prices low. Meanwhile, the United Russia Party had collapsed in the wake of yet another financial scandal, forcing Vladimir Putin, Father of the Nation, freshly released from house arrest, to step down from public life.

Soon after Putin's enforced retirement, Kazakhstan had withdrawn from the Customs Union with Russia and Belarus, joining with the fundamentalist Mohammedans aligned with the Council of God based in Mecca. Russia, already expelled from the World Trade Organization at the insistence of the Israeli Prime Minister and a coalition of international business leaders, was now essentially blackmailed into becoming a signatory to the Transatlantic Trade and Investment Partnership, effectively allowing the seizure of Russian assets in lieu of unpaid debts. Within days of the WTO announcement, the UN had imposed food and trade embargoes in response to the Kremlin's continued opposition to its humanitarian missions in eastern Ukraine. All economic indices showed Russia to be in an economic crisis far deeper than it had faced in the last decade of the twentieth century. Taking advantage of Moscow's geopolitical weakness, Brussels had forced a revision to the 2010 delineation of the Norwegian-Russian Arctic Maritime border, giving the EU greater access to the oil and gas fields on the sea bed. The Organisation for Security and Cooperation in Europe began stating openly that it would fund Alexei Navalny's Progress Party as reports of irregularities at 50 percent of polling stations during the last elections emerged.

Tom felt nervous as he strode towards the winking light signalling his turn at the immigration desk. He was not sure what kind of reception he would receive. The world was changed now. He was thinking of all those old clichés, like Checkpoint Charlie in Berlin, or being dragged off by stern-faced men in crumpled suits for questioning. It was very clear that Professor Hunter was no Harry Palmer. He had read Len Deighton and Le Carr é, and his first experience of Russian bureaucracy played right into Western preconceptions. Brutal Formica faces reflected on the shiny tabletops. There was a plethora of forms that needed to be completed in triplicate, stamped, and sanctioned. The former Eastern Bloc still seemed to be living in the shadow of the Wall. An Iron Curtain separated the new breed of capitalists from *Homo Sovieticus*.

Given clearance, he made his way to baggage handling, past keen-eyed security and customs staff, out to a lemon-lit foyer where circulating conveyor belts chugged consumptively, spewing shrink-wrapped luggage close to the taxi ranks. There were all sorts of bemused and confused people milling around. He saw the excited and tired meeting of relatives and friends. There was patrolling militia in high-vis jackets, Kalashnikovs looped lazily over their shoulders, gun barrels pointing at chipped floor tiles. Outbound passengers wandered about, faces scanning electronic screens, watching the intermittent updates for connections. Long-separated couples rushed to embrace. Frosty fathers returning from business trips gave guilty gifts to their children in full view of beaming babushkas overwhelmed with emotion at the sight of their daughters re-united with their errant husbands before the winter ice storms set in.

Tom's attention was caught by a news-flash about a gun attack in Omsk. He gripped his brown leather case and meandered after a Karelian couple walking towards the *'to the city'* sign. Standing on the cracked pavement of the concourse, he realised there would be no welcoming committee from his contacts in the Borean Alliance. He had not really expected one. Not even vocal protests from Black Bloc youths waving a 'Go home British Fascist' banner. Controversy had followed him ever since his work on the Septentrion Project antagonised the Antifa mobsters. They had disrupted his lectures and burned his books after he came out as an outspoken supporter of the British guerrillas fighting alongside the French Resistance against the newly-imposed Eurabist Regime in Paris. At the same time, his warnings about the North African Federation of Muslim Nations fomenting civil unrest in Central Asia had not been overlooked. He received unpleasant calls in the middle of the night and death threats from crazed zealots operating out of ghettos in the north of England.

Tom had long harboured the suspicion that because the Slavs had escaped most of the corrosive influence of political correctness, they would act as a catalyst for a White revolution. For years following the murder of a Russian boy whilst defending his girlfriend from molestation by immigrants in the Moscow district of Biryulovo, thousands of marchers had come out on the streets, carrying Romanov flags on National Unity Day, screaming *'Rossiia est sviataia Rus!'* The war in Donbass and the clarion call to Muslims in Tajikistan, Turkmenistan, Abkhazia, Kazakhstan, and Dagestan to join their brothers in a jihad had polarised communities from Novgorod to Tomsk. There was a real threat to internal stability now that the Russian army had been pushed back over the Terek River in Chechnya, and both the European Union and the United Nations were set to recognise the Free Republic of Ichkeria.

Radical forces, predominantly made up of disgruntled and poorly-educated Balkars, Abkhaz, North Caucasians, Tartars, Bashkias, and fundamentalist Turks were being joined by Arabs and Africans fighting under the banners of the Al-Nusra Front, Hizb-ut-Tahrir, Akromiya, Gulen, Tovba, Azerbaijani Jamaat, and Al Shabaab. The bazaars of Argun, Ashgabat, Baku, and Osh were filled with military hardware supplied by the oil-rich Gulf states. Armies of young Muslims in camouflage jackets, fired up by hysterical rhetoric about killing the *kuffar*, were being trained in the Ferghana and Rasht valleys.

Already there were gun battles between groups of Jeyshulla, Soldiers of Allah, and local security forces on the streets of Armavir in Krasnodar Krai, Mumbai-style attacks on hotels in Sochi, and Dagestani militants laying siege to the Ossetian capital of Vladikavkaz. Schoolchildren had been burnt alive in Buynaksk. Afghanistan, Pakistan, and Iraq were acting as base camps for sedition. Salafist money paying for the new *madrasah* schools opening in Perm, Samara, and Nadym. The whole frontier across Chechnya, Ingushetia, Kabardino-Balkaria, and North Ossetia-Alania was aflame.

Within Russia itself, self-segregation, suspicion, and open hostility was breaking out in previously peaceful communities. The bitter memory of the bombings on the Nevsky Express and Moscow Metro were still fresh in people's minds, as were those in Kizlar, Stavropol, Domodedovo, and Volgograd. Now there was the slaughter of Russian families in Nazran, the torching of Orthodox churches in Kazan, and acid attacks on blonde women in Ekaterinburg. The rantings of Al Qaeda leaders declaring that 'anyone who prays and fasts but advocates parliamentary democracy are apostates' had been painted on the walls of churches in Noril'sk. Mosques were filled to the brim. Guns, ammunition, and heroin passed from hand to hand under the cover of darkness.

Tom was mildly irritated that his arrival did not warrant vocal opposition from the Left, but he quickly dismissed such feelings as petty vanity as he stood waiting patiently for his ride. Beaten-up Volga saloons with hanging doors and dangling wing mirrors drew up next to sleek limousines. No class distinction here, he laughed silently to himself. The new models purred like warm panthers on the prowl. The older vehicles' ball bearings grated like knives on stone. Drivers stood out in the rain, smoking, joking, and staring at the slim-rimmed girls as they passed, pushing luggage in screech-wheeled trolleys, ignoring the wolf whistles, refraining from making eye contact with the lecherous loiterers. Tom saw two blue trails of beer breath punctuate the night air. He was looking for someone looking for him. Then he saw the red tip of a cigarette's glow, rising on the intake and fading on the exhale, disappearing slowly into the headlight's gloaming.

Roman had picked him out and peeled away from his gaggle of leather-jacketed Jacobins and their tiresome conversation about the price of BMW spares. He flicked his cigarette, a fire-fly fizz of light in a sheen of petroleum. Taking Professor Hunter's suitcase in his firm grip, he clumsily shook hands with the other.

'Good evening', Roman said in strained English. 'Please, my car.' Tom noticed the Gromoviti Znaci thunder flash badge on Roman's collar as he slid into the passenger seat. He realised almost immediately that the slack on the safety belt rendered the harness useless. Officious policemen walked past in big hats and stretched uniforms. They were Russian Gary Coopers, sauntering self-importantly, scratched leather holsters riding high on their hips. The new arrival wondered if they would use their VUL pistols or run at the first sight of an Avar with a scimitar. Roman slammed the trunk closed, jumped in behind the wheel, and fired up the engine. 'No belt!' he said, shaking his head. He pulled out onto the near-side lane of Pulkovskoe Shosse, edging into traffic back towards Moskovskiy Prospekt.

The road was a tan leather whiplash. Wheels sprayed mud, and cancerous trees stood like skin-scratching sentinels, marking the car's progress. Tom noticed how the lethargic march of white birch was sometimes interrupted by electricity pylons, metallic stalagmites set stark against the blanched skyline. Roman aimed straight ahead, following a clear path under the overhang of dying branches and dripping cables. His cigarette rolled back and forth along the narrow crack between his clamped lips. Yevgeny Nikitin blared out the speakers, a crescendo of guitars and the singer's conservatoire-trained voice spliced by the spo-

radic sweep of squeaking wipers. The headlights of oncoming cars washed over hoardings, adverts for mobile
phones, and high-tech gadgetry. Occasionally, a back ripple of exhausted light would catch on the chipped edges
of the miniature icons decorating Roman's dashboard,
setting off a glint of gold, torpid yellow washing over the
two fixed expressions staring back at them from the dark
windscreen.

Tom was going through his pockets, checking the au-
thorisation on his entry visa, recalling the surly face at
passport control. He had recoiled at the inky thud of the
stamp, still picturing the pretty young girl in the small cu-
bicle behind the screen, tight green uniform, yellow braid
and pure white complexion. She had those judgemental
eyes that ran like a scalpel through your scrotal sack. 'No
secrets, absolutely no secrets here', they seemed to whisper. 'We have rules and you will abide by them!' That click
of the authoritarian heel was still resonating as the car
swept by a statue of Lenin. The dictator's stiff arm pointed
forward to a bright proletarian future. A brave new world
without kulaks. Professor Hunter surveyed the cold
bronze figure, deliberately set back off the road in order to
intimidate, standing amid the colonnades of the old party
headquarters. Arrogant and haughty, Comrade Vladimir
Iliyich's slanted eyes, bald head, and goatee glistened under a crescent arc of light. There was no doubting his tribal lineage.

'How far to city?' he asked.

'*Nyet?*' came back the reply.

'Hotel?' Tom supplemented the word with Esperanto
gestures signifying the cutting of food and sleeping on a
pillow. Roman's unshaven jaw broke into a grill-toothed
smile.

'*Da!*' He lit another cigarette, offered the ragged end of
the pack to Tom, who declined with a tentative '*Nyet*' of
his own. The driver laughed loudly.

'*Gorad!*' he pointed. Tom shook his head. 'English?' he
continued. 'London, Big Ben, the Beatles.' This time it was

Tom's turn to laugh.

'*Da*, Leningrad, Peterhof, Putin!'

'*Da, da, da!*' Well, it was communication of a sort, the Professor convinced himself, even if it was a touch primitive. As they drove further, the post-war office blocks and shabby Khrushchovka apartments lining the avenues began to thin out, and the crumbling teeth of nineteenth-century mansions and onion-domed churches stood out against the sparkle of silver starlight. Blue- and ochre-fronted streets sat astride hump-backed bridges. Their nocturnal journey led them further towards the centre, penetrating deeper and deeper into a cobweb of fading baroque stonework and moonlit canals.

Tom could not shake the feeling that people were standing on the upper floors of the Italianate facades, dark glass eyes spying on the vast squares filled with mounted bronze horsemen and wrought-iron railings. Cafés and bars were full to bursting. People's faces contorted with laughter, cigarettes fencing in gesticulating fingers. He was witnessing a nation in denial, his imagination chilled by the thought of the Mongol hordes gathering once again, ready to overwhelm Holy Russia.

Lines of pedestrians crossing the Voznesenskiy caused the traffic to stack. Teenage carousers with armfuls of liquor sang and danced on both sides of the road. Two young blondes clip-clopped by on chestnut horses, linear bodies projecting elongated silhouettes from the bulbous streetlights onto the front of the Mariinskiy Palace. Tom could just make out the great golden dome of St Isaac's Cathedral looming like a dirty iceberg, all marble and grimy granite, filling the night sky ahead.

'Hotel?' he asked hopefully.

'Astoria', Roman replied, pulling up sharp in front of a gang of drunken students criss-crossing the road, falling about, making general nuisances of themselves.

'They seem to be having fun', the Englishman muttered irritatedly to himself. Fingers tapped the roof of the car. Nervously he opened the window, only to be confronted by what he took to be the beaming face of God's most favoured angel, passing him a bottle of Altai vodka. He hesitated. She threw back her long brown hair and said something Tom assumed was encouragement. Roman nodded.

'Blue label is good', the driver confirmed. In a bid to seem hospitable, the reluctant Professor had a long swig, almost immediately suffering the hot needle stab of pure alcohol as it thrust its poisonous blade deep into his liver. Eyes watering, he coughed uncontrollably, tongue swelling like an aroused penis, its hard, red tip throbbing inside his throat, causing him to gag.

'Welcome to Russia', his beautiful benefactor laughed in perfect American-English.

The Astoria squatted like a fat brown bullfrog on the corner of the square, red awnings jutting like giant eyelids. It had once been the most fashionable hotel in pre-revolutionary St Petersburg. It was the location from where M15 had plotted to assassinate Rasputin, and was the scene of a famous last stand by the White Cadets against the Reds. After the Bolshevik Revolution, Lenin hosted the Second Communist International there. Later, the British Fabian writer and Slavophile H G Wells was a regular visitor.

Roman helped Tom carry his luggage into the plush lobby. Once there, he stepped aside, making a call on his mobile to confirm his passenger's safe arrival. The driver talked quickly, while Tom checked in, only halting to receive further instructions. After completing registration Tom, handed over his passport. Then Roman passed him the Nokia so he could speak to his host.

'It's Grigori from the International Forum', croaked a fractured voice down an intermittent line.

'*Privet*, Grigori! It's Tom. Yes, a good flight . . . Roman got me here on time, no problem . . . Yes, one hour will be fine. I just need to shower and shave . . . The Sakura . . . A car will pick me up, where? At the door, *horosho* . . . See you there . . . '

Tom slipped Roman thirty crisp US dollars, and there

was a moment of male discomfort before they hugged. Professor Hunter pointed to the Gromoviti Znaci badge. '*Tovarich*', he insisted.

'*Dobre*', Roman announced loudly, 'Russki way!' With a slap on the shoulder they parted as friends. Roman returned to his familiar routine on the dirty streets of the congested city, while his new comrade went to a third-floor suite to freshen up before an urgent appointment with Russia's political opposition.

Tom had a clear view over St Isaac's Square. The city centre was aglow with honking cars, flashing headlights, and constant foot traffic. He dropped his case and pulled off his shirt and tie. Swallowing the complementary chocolates decorating his pillow, he sat on the corner of the bed, removing his Loake handmade shoes and cashmere socks. The carpet's luxurious thickness felt reassuring after his long flight. Opening the suitcase, he lifted a copy of Alexander Dugin's *The Eurasian Mission: An Introduction to Neo-Eurasianism*, which had been printed by Arktos, as well as a well-fingered copy of American socialist John Reed's 1919 classic about the October Revolution, *Ten Days That Shook the World*. Placing the opposing texts at juxtapositions on the bedside table, he reached for his washbag, peeled off his sticky underwear, and wandered into the ensuite.

The plastic shower curtain slid easily on its rail, luke-warm water sputtering from the groaning nozzle. He felt his age as the spray cascaded over stiff shoulders, soapy bubbles trickling down pale thighs. Travelling economy did that to him. Aches and pains, real or imaginary, shot though his body. Running gel between his fingers, he washed his hair, memories of the cramped plane melting away with the citrus tang wafting from the open bottle.

Stepping out onto marble tiles, wrapped in Egyptian cotton, he lathered his face and reached for a cut-throat razor. His slate-grey eyes looked tired as he drew the blade over a stubbled chin. He stood for a few seconds admiring his chest in the mirror, steamy droplets running over chrome, posing self-consciously, picking the most favourable angle. Swimming and bench-pressing kept his stomach wall tight and firm. Middle age was a battle he could rightfully claim to be winning. But some days were better than others, and he knew he was reaching the tipping point.

Tom always laid out his toiletries with a military precision that would have made von Clausewitz proud. Vitamin tablets and cod liver oil were set at a thirty degree angle from his hand cream. The blue body lotion was like a rook in a Bobby Fischer chess match, ready to sweep down the channel between the taps. A half-empty bottle of Terre D'Hermes glinted in the mirror light. His fingers smelled of fresh *eau de cologne*. His cheeks were stinging as he slapped the tincture onto smarting skin.

Standing in his bathrobe, twisting the top off a bottle of Perrier, he bent and sniffed at the bouquet of seasonal flowers. The message from Grigori read, 'Welcome to Piter'. The room was a generous double. Pulling the red velvet curtains over his view of the Cathedral, he began combing his fair hair in the large mirror, noting the first threads of grey, reflecting philosophically that they offered the potential for a distinguished look. The sort of academic gravitas he longed for. Climbing into a Hugo Boss suit, fresh white shirt and claret tie, he was like a chevalier putting on his armour. Black cufflinks engraved with silver hagal runes gleamed in the half-light. Shiny Italian shoes and an Omega co-axial chronometer wristwatch completed the ensemble. Tom felt like a Nietzschean Overman in designer suits. Adrenalin levels began to rise. Moving to the door, checking the time with an elegant twist of his wrist, he caught himself saying to the empty room, 'Five minutes early, perfect!'

In the hallway, he caught the sound of multilingual matrimonial arguments through half-closed doorways. The familiar hum of domestic discord narrated his journey to the top of the grand stairwell. For a moment he thought of his own failed marriage. Cecilia had never understood him, what had really moved and motivated him. And what moved and motivated her, disgusted him. The product of a middle-class military family and an exclusive boarding school, she was geared to sibling rivalry, the bigger house, better car, and the executive career in marketing. When his studies into group evolutionary theory began to make his lectures controversial amongst the faculty, she worried more about his promotional prospects, rather than the validity of his theory. Tom's favourable critiques of Vladimir Avdeyev's *Rasologia* and the *Biblioteka Rasovoy Mysli* made him about as popular as Arthur Jensen and Glade Whitney amongst the politically correct crowd at the academy. 'Why doesn't Dean Meyer like you?' she hissed, harridan style. 'We never get invited to his soirees!' For months she had lacerated him with her box-cutter tongue. Then, one morning, while he was giving a class on Hans Eysenk, Cecilia had slipped away, leaving her solicitor's business card and some scorch marks from a spilled coffee on the dining room table.

He hit the touch pad and rode the mirrored elevator to the ground floor. Emerging from sliding glass doors, Tom thought he caught an admiring glance off the pretty redhead at reception. A bespectacled doorman in a powder-blue waistcoat watched him coming from the far end of the bustling lobby. With perfect timing, he bowed and pulled on the brass handle, letting in a gush of cold night air. The Englishman thanked him and stepped out onto the stone-angled corner of Bolshaya Morskaya.

A hotel car sat waiting, graphite and chrome in the pale wash of the foyer's roof light. The barrel-chested driver made sure his passenger was safely belted before pulling out into traffic. They had not gone far before they stalled in a jam on the Pereulok Antonenko, just a little short of the Griboedova. A battered yellow street cab squeezed in alongside. The Mongol driver pressed hard on his horn. 'Just like Milan', Tom said under his breath. Vehicles edged forward, cutting each other up, trying to force their way into gaps before they closed.

Ten minutes later, the knot broke free. Cars were moving slowly past a broken-down Zhiguli 1500, bonnet lifted, its dead metal carcass lying flat like an old carthorse on the side of the road. A young family stood bereft, the blonde wife remonstrating with her husband, a crying infant in her arms.

'Rubbish!' his driver spat. Tom did not respond, unsure if he would be subjected to a tirade about how bad things were now, as opposed to the *nouveau riche* Russia of a decade earlier. The chauffeur had already shared his views on how normal Russians were hurrying to change their savings and pensions into furniture and jewellery. Tom was imagining scenes reminiscent of the bread queues of the early '90s as they listened to the car's radio. An interview was being conducted by Benny Efrati for RIA Novosti with the new Governor of Russia's Central Bank, indicating that the economic situation was reaching 'super-critical':

- ❖ The Russian Central Bank raises interest rates by 18 percent as a 'shock and awe' tactic to stem the tide, but fails to tame the market;
- ❖ George Soros re-emphasises his case, made a few years previously, that the West should see this return to *Smutnoye Vremya*, a time of troubles, as a precursor to open warfare;
- ❖ EU bankers escalate their economic leverage as a means to force Russia into accepting western Ukraine as a part of the NATO sphere of influence.

They pulled up in a narrow side-street near the water. Stragglers sauntered on both sides of the canal, heading back towards Nevsky after enjoying the Orthodox Choir at the Church of the Spilled Blood. Giant onion domes stood out against the stars, casting deep purple bruises over the stone embankment. He noticed a beautiful young couple standing hand-in hand-on a wrought-iron bridge. They embraced passionately. An old man cycled by, thin metal wheels rattling on chipped cobbles.

Tom stood at the driver's window trying to negotiate the return trip. Getting nowhere, he twisted away, walking through the crowd, his body, along with many others, reflected in the burning translucence of a passing canal boat's windows.

His initial impression was that the Sakura was anything but remarkable, a single neon sign hooked crookedly on a plain cement wall. He stepped down into the dimly-lit entrance and was quickly swallowed by the wide throat of a sunken stairwell. Pushing on the door, he entered, silver globes strobing the faces of guests as they swilled sake, rang forks on wine glasses, and called for birthday toasts.

He was name-checked by a demure kimono-clad waitress who took his coat, leading him through a tight tangle of drunken patrons. Credit cards were being swiped and handfuls of crumpled notes were clipped into a snapping cash register. Tom tripped along behind the diminutive Oriental through dense cigarette smoke to an alcove where Grigori was waiting with three other guests, two middle-aged men and a young woman.

'*Privet,* Professor Hunter', he shouted excitedly, leaping up from behind a low table, hugging the new arrival in two bear-like arms. Tom identified the smell of pirated French cologne and imported cigars. '*Shto u vas jes t'vypit?*' The Englishman looked bemused, but before he could excuse his poor Russian, Grigori corrected himself. 'Sorry', he laughed with his trademark belly bawl, 'What would you like to drink?'

'Beer?' Grigori ordered a Heineken. 'That is good beer', he promised with a wicked wink. 'It's brewed locally!' More laughter.

Turning his giant crocodile smile on the others, Grigori introduced Svetlana, a blonde, Germanic-looking girl with searching blue eyes and a voice like percolating coffee. She had been a research assistant to Alexander Dugin, former

Head of the Sociology of International Relations Department at Moscow State University. It also transpired that she was a specialist in the political philosophy of Eurasianist thinkers like the linguist N S Trubetskoy, the geographer P N Savitsky, and G V Florovsky. Hunter took her hand respectfully. 'And this is Dimitry, he is a freelance writer whose father was involved with *Samizdat*, *Nash sovremennik*, and Veche in the old days.' Dimitry was an immaculately turned-out little man with a firm handshake and crisply lacquered white hair. 'You may be familiar with his works on VSKHSON's corporate state philosophy and the political doctrine of Danilevski, Struve, and Ilyin?'

'I am delighted to meet you', he said in broken English, 'I am a great admirer of your work on Russian conservatism, and particularly your essay on Shafarevich's *Russophobia.*'

'The pleasure is all mine', Tom replied. 'I read your excellent thesis on Solonevich.' Then, collecting his beer from the waiter, he reached out to Grigori's third guest, Alexander, a publisher of Pan-Slavic and occult journals.

'I think we have a mutual hero?' Alexander suggested. 'I know you admire Michael Freeman, who translated *The Book of Vles.*'

'Small world, I just read Chivilikhin's *Pamyat!*'

'The world is getting smaller all the time', Grigori said conspiratorially as they settled down to eat from a melange of enamel bowls. 'Knife and fork, or chopsticks?'

'Sticks', Tom confirmed. 'After all, when in Rome.' This made the Russians laugh.

'We use fingers', Alexander chortled.

'I have never been to Rome', Dimitry grinned, 'but I think they like sushi there too, no?'

'It's a world-wide phenomenon', the Englishman confirmed. 'Indian and Chinese cuisine is even more popular than roast beef and boiled potatoes in my country.'

'Surely not better than fish and chips', boomed Grigori, bragging loudly to all in earshot. 'When I was in London I ate fish and chips in Trafalgar Square, right under Nelson's column. It tasted marvellous, even better with all the pigeon shit!'

❖ Prominent French politician Said Be Hassi travels to Moscow to chair a meeting between Orthodox and Muslim faith groups;

❖ Russian military forces become increasingly ineffective, working out of a dwindling number of bases across the Ob;

❖ The land west of the Taz and east of the Tobol rivers becomes known as Ma wara al-nahr, the new Trans-oxiana;

❖ Vladivostok's Oriental Institute is renamed for the Islamic scientist, Abu Nasr al-Muhammad al-Farabi;

❖ A great revival in the philosophical works of Abu Ali Ibn Sina, known to the West as Avicenna, sees copies of his books roll off newly-established Islamic printing presses in Kostroma and Tula;

❖ 'The Soviet *kolkhoze-haust*, sometimes spoken of kindly as collectivisations of a hundred years ago, led to the genocide of a third of our people. They closed mosques and arrested our *ulema*. But it was the Kazakhs who made up Panfilov's men who stopped the Germans tanks outside Moscow! It was Sultan Baimagambetov who saved Leningrad! Ghani Safiullin who won Stalingrad! And it was Rakhimzan Koshkarbayev who raised the Red Flag over the Reichstag. And now it will be the Oral-men's army that that seizes Orenburg and Omsk for the Nurli Zhol', said Maxat Sarinzhipov, the new Kazakh President, speaking from the Temple of Peace, a sixty-two-metre-high pyramid in Astana;

❖ Sarinzhipov, holder of the Kurmet Order, declares his country's borders open between China, Uzbekistan, Turkmenistan, and Russia. 'There should be no need for visas at Maikapchagai, Chongkapra,

Kolzhat, Karkara, Aisha Bibi, Sypatai Batyr, and Khorgos. No barriers between brothers!';

❖ Within months, the Kazakhstan Khanate announces that provocations by Rus separatists, disciples of Viktor Kazimirchuck in Kazakhstan's border regions, has necessitated special forces seizing Kazakh-Russian border crossings at Roslavka, Taskala, Ust-Kamenogorsk, and Semipalatinsk. Justifying his country's actions, Sarinzhipov said, 'As a consequence of these security measures, we are guaranteeing safe passage of migrants from the east as part of our humanitarian mission';

❖ In response to questions posed by the Russian authorities in Krasnoyarsk Krai, the President said, 'Kazakhstan has long been a crossing point between east and west. What is different now?';

❖ The Trans-Caucasian Federative model is abandoned in favour of independent tribal Caliphates;

❖ Within weeks, new laws are introduced expelling ethnic Russians, Germans, and others from their homes in Karaganda, Pavlodar, Akmola, and Kostanay;

❖ Plaques commemorating the Russian and Kazakh intellectuals Dostoevsky and Chokan Valikhanov are torn down in Petropavlovsk. Monuments to Pushkin are replaced by those of Abai Kunanbaev;

❖ Urban guerrillas fighting for Novarossiya in Oskemen are seized and executed at the foot of the Bayterek Tower in Astana;

❖ Latin inscriptions carved by Roman centurions in the first century AD, indicating Azerbaijan was the previous eastern frontier of Europe, are destroyed by acid attack.

They talked through the evening. Each took turns raising the traditional toast of Russian intellectuals, 'Let us drink to the success of our hopeless cause!' Chopsticks danced, teeth gnashed on salad and seaweed garnish.

Glycerine-brown trails of glutinous slug-blood dotted bowls of soy sauce.

Replete, Grigori sat back, mountainous in his lugubrious joy. He was a committed member of several political groupings, including the Slavyansky Soyuz Nationalist Movement and the Izborsky Club. Clever like a fox, his eyes surveyed the body language of each of his little reception party and their unguarded personal interactions. Tom recognised how Grigori orchestrated the conversation, sometimes with a venomous appeal to base instincts, other times with deft poetic phrases. His lips jitterbugged with humorous anecdotes.

'Listen', Grigori said over brandy and coffee. 'It is good we come together because this is a very serious business.' They all shuffled expectantly in their seats. 'The truth is we can no longer speak as freely as we once did. Babel is set to introduce laws to silence opposition. Our brother Egor Kholmogorov, editor of *Russian Surveyor*, famed for applauding the removal of the Yanukovych regime, was hospitalised after a mysterious altercation on the street. Soon we will be back to the days of Soviet soup kitchens and doors being kicked in during the night. Our influence is limited, and time is running out. These last elections were a pantomime. Dugin's Eurasian Party could never hold together. We all know who is pulling the strings. Who is at the back of all this financial turmoil. It is the same people who manipulate the White House, the EU, and the UN. Our people need true leadership, not presidents and prime ministers who play musical chairs while NATO surrounds us with missiles and EU troops prepare to enter our near abroad. I mean, just look at Ukraine. Washington, Brussels, and Tel Aviv are the real enemy, not our Slavic brothers in Kiev. It is *divide et impera* by the same people who are selling Europe out to the Muslims of Pakistan and the dark hordes of northern Africa.' Then, in an aside to Tom, he said, 'Is that how you see it?'

'Yes, a case of divide and conquer', Tom affirmed. 'Prime Minister Cameron even sent British military advisers there at the request of his rabbinical brothers.'

Grigori continued, 'The Third Rome is under siege. Not just from the West but also from the East. What we need is a Moscow, Minsk, and Kiev axis unifying Slavs, not dividing them. Damn Astana's steppe bandits and all of Eurasia, I say. We all know what is happening in the Caucasus. They are calling for the establishment of a Caliphate. Even as we sit here, the reformed Sassanid Army led by the Caliph Harum al-Rashid Division pushes on the Derbent Gates, the entry point into the Eurasian Steppe. Where did all these people come from? Have you been to Irkutsk recently?

❖ The Tbilisi Trade Accords: a delegation from the Organisation for Economic Co-operation and Development (OECD) composed of American, EU, Chinese, Islamic Federation, and Israeli representatives meet with the newly-elected Russian President following the collapse of the Eurasian Economic Community to agree to the division of Russia into four distinct economic trading areas: namely the Slavic, European Russia, lying in the Volga basin and linked to New York and Brussels; Caucasian Russia, between the Black and Caspian seas, linked to Istanbul and Baku; and the Ural and Siberian Russia, linked to Astana and Beijing;

❖ Ancient Lake Baikal, in eastern Siberia, the world's largest freshwater resource, is claimed by China, which immediately begins draining its 23,000 cubic kilometres of water from Angara to supply the growing population of the Sino-Siberian hinterland;

❖ The Sino-Muslim Development Treaty bans Russian industrialists from the strategic Altai mountain range where the borders of Russia, China, Mongolia, and Kazakhstan intersect, apportioning the land at the headwaters of the Irtysh, Orb, and the Sayan down to the Gobi to the Altaic family of

nations;
* ❖ Major industrialisation begins on the Uvs, Khyargas, Drogon, and Khar watercourses.

'If we do not link up with the rest of the White world, Siberia will be lost forever. The government has abandoned the country. There are only seven million Russians now, compared to the hundred million in China's most northeastern province. Our people have to defend themselves. The 18th Machine Gun Artillery Division was completely over-run in Irkutsk. I have witnessed the mass movement of six hundred thousand illegals through the border. And now the Islamic Uighur separatists of Xinjiang are committing suicide bombings in markets and stabbing people on railway platforms. It is a tidal wave of human material, I tell you, flooding along the Tunguska and the Kolyma. It is a new Mongol yoke that will make the time of Ghengis Khan's *yasa* look like Christmas holidays.' His audience became anxious. 'You know, there is a story my uncle told me about a closed lecture he attended many years ago with a functionary of the Foreign Ministry. When someone in the audience answered that capitalist imperialism was still the greatest threat to socialism, he laughed contemptuously. It is China, he shouted. To postpone dealing with the Chinese problem is especially dangerous because time is on their side, and the longer we or the West waits, the more difficult this problem will become.'

'And we have waited far too long', Svetlana said. 'Business agreements between Rosneft and Sinopec are worthless. The Chinese model is the destruction of any other national element. They plunder our land east of the Lena and strip the wood from the taigas, drain the water from Lake Balkhash and siphon oil from under the Tien Shan mountains. Gone are the days when Russian and Kazakh youth shared café tables in Almaty. Now they are split into ethnic gangs. Using mercantilism, the Chinese intend to restore their Qing dynasty in Mongolia while hoovering

up the Gobi Desert's minerals. Ulan Bator is owned by Beijing. There are military skirmishes from the Kyrgyz border
to Vladivostok. We either cede land or face open hostility.
They already outproduce us in manufacturing using their
Laogai sweatshops, and commit genetic genocide against
suppressed peoples such as the Tibetans by forced inter-
marriage.'

'Yes, they are not just after the zinc, nickel, tin, and
precious metals. Long-legged Siberian girls are already
bearing sons with Chinese faces. We fooled ourselves that
our own Turkic element would outgrow their infantile
belief system. While we are divided amongst Neo-
Slavophiles, Eurasianists, National Communists, and ethnic nationalists, they are united by their Noble Qur'an.
Our heartland stretches from Moscow to the Urals, and
then to the Transbaikal. But look at the foreign faces
swamping our streets. Listen to the different languages
children speak in our schools. Now there is a civil war just
like in France, Italy, and those other countries!' Dimitry
sounded angry. 'We need another victory like at Kulikovo.'
Grigori cheered indignantly.

'Our government is full of appeasers, paralysed with
fear', said Alexander through cigarette smoke. 'Under the
Soviets there were over forty-five ethnic regions. By the
time of the 1989 census, more than four hundred different
ethnicities were within our borders.'

'There were plenty of signs years ago. Remember the
Nord-Ost siege? Who do you think blew up the Moscow
to St Petersburg train line and Domodedovo airport?'
Grigori stuttered, spilling a mouthful of cognac. Tom
shrugged his shoulders. 'The same people who set off ex-
plosives on your underground?'

'And Madrid and *Charlie Hebdo!*' Svetlana insisted.

'No, Paris might have been others', Grigori hinted.

'We never recovered from the *marazm*', Dimitry muttered. 'There are too many nostalgics for the Soviet empire.'

'He means the Breznhev sterility', Svetlana added for

Tom's benefit.

'No, no!' Grigori laughed. 'Sterility means no sperm for babies. You mean senility.' Then, tapping a finger against the side of his head, 'No brain power!'

'The same result', she smiled back sarcastically over the rim of her coffee cup.

'But since Putin's 2006 natalist strategy of giving maternity money to families, your birth-rate is slowly stabilising', Tom interjected, completely misunderstanding the point his co-conspirators were making. 'In the UK our population growth is fuelled by Third World immigrants!'

'Russian faces in strollers is good!' Grigori confirmed. 'The old President even enacted anti-homosexual laws and called abortion an abomination.'

'Don't give him too much credit, he was a power-hungry, self-interested politician, no different from the EU bureaucrats', insisted Alexander.

'But at least Putin declared that Russians have a unique and very powerful genetic code', affirmed Dimitry.

'Interesting that it was Khodorkovsky who challenged that', Sveta said decisively.

'And the very reason why he was the Soros Foundation's Man of the Year for financing the Russian Liberty and Freedom Party', Grigori belched.

'Another bloodsucking flea, just like Boris Berezovsky. But at least that one had the decency to hang himself.'

'Or was hung?' Sveta propositioned.

'It is all about money!' Alexander raised a glass. 'To Sergei Yevgenevich!' Tom looked uncertain.

'Former Chairman of the State Duma', Grigori explained.

'There was a book', Dimitry said. '*Another Life*, published many years ago by the underground. My economics colleagues used to quote at me from it . . . "If nothing changes you and your children will continue to scurry around in shops, wear faded clothes, wait in line for an apartment for ten years . . ."'

'I've never read it', Sveta breathed, 'but like Zhirinovsky

said, the Americans are clever. They knew it is better to
come here with chewing gum, stockings, and McDon-
ald's.'

'I didn't read it either', blurted Dimitry, 'but it is irrele-
vant now, Khodorkovsky's book, *Man with a Rouble*, out-
sells it. Anyway, we should all be reading Dmitry Orlov's
Five Stages of Collapse or Dugin's *Mysteries of Eurasia* and
Foundations of Geopolitics, and writers like Aleseev.'

'Dimitry is right. Naishul's book has long passed its
sell-by date', Grigori insisted. 'Alexei was a child when that
book was circulating. Khodorkovsky's is a celebration of
embezzlement. At least Orlov was born in this city. Since
then, mafia capitalists have been let loose by the shock-
therapy economics of Gaidar, Fyodorov, and Chubais.
Then, when the American ideas they used failed, we
turned to Chernomyrdin and Gerashchenko's liberal credit system. The World Bank estimated something like forty
billion dollars was made on the back of sell-offs and ac-
quisitions by racketeers between 1991 and 1994 alone. We
had a choice back then, either to join those who exploit
the world economically, or oppose them. This generation
lives in a world where five years ago there were more bil-
lionaires in Moscow than New York. Have you seen
Tverskaya Street recently? Once, there were better clothes
there than on Rodeo Drive. Italian shoes and Swiss watches are not the answer. We need our spirit back.' His hands
moved in karate chops before his face. 'We need *pas-
sionarnost!*'

'Not so long ago we had all the gas', said Sveta ironical-
ly. 'Gazprom still holds reserves in Kazahkstan, Turkmenistan, and Uzbekistan.'

'But for how long? It is the energy resources the Muslims are seeking to control', countered Tom. 'They will
nationalise those assets and refuse to acknowledge Russian ownership. Will Beijing still honour your trade deals?
The EU is just waiting until they can seize all the minerals
in the north. The South Stream project was once going to
supply 64 billion cubic metres of gas to Europe, but the

price of energy is being manipulated.'

'Tom is right', Grigori said. 'The Chinese are devious and cannot be trusted. There is also a powerful alien grip on the American mind. Our enemies still want to impose an encirclement, the Anaconda Thesis on us. The EU's *Ostpolitik* is to talk of a new Iron Curtain because of Russian aggression in Donetsk, then pull that curtain down with a bang. Even one of our own parliamentarians, Vladimir Ryzhkov, said the EU is the most successful model in history. NATO troops are now in Hungary, Romania, Bulgaria, Lithuania, Latvia, and Estonia. They join with Wall Street to intervene in Kazakhstan and Azerbaijan. They desire Georgia's gold, copper, timber, and to choke the Baku-Tbilisi-Ceyhan pipeline, investing billions on a euro-transport corridor through Turkey, via the Caspian, to China. For God's sake, they overthrew the legal government of Serbia. Bombed our brothers in Belgrade. Installed Muslims in Bosnia. Look closely at events in Ukraine. The US National Security Adviser, Zbigniew Brzezinski, said, 'Ukraine's very existence as an independent country transforms Russia.' The EU is in bed with oligarchs like Ihor Kolomoisky to raise volunteer battalions in Dnipropetrovsk. Jews like him and Arseniy Yatsenyuk are shouting about another Holocaust and how the Rabbis of the Golden Rose are leading the Chosen in yet another exodus to Mariupol. The American sanctions hurt us. The hand of Soros and the CIA are behind this? The USA has reappointed Victoria Nuland, Secretary of State for European and Eurasian Affairs, who wants to buy Ukraine on the cheap, offering a few billion. Before all this, Russia offered 15 billion, joint projects involving heavy industry and setting gas prices below the market value. I say, God bless those burnt to death in Odessa, the slaughtered innocents in Slovyansk, Zakharchenko, and the defenders of Donetsk! They shelled the shit out of Horlivka, then shot down the Malaysian airways MH17 in a false flag operation. Why do you think they want to dislodge our influence from the Carpathians and undermine us in Belarus with the Treaty of Nice and their offer of Eastern Partnership? Where do the pipelines run? Which tribe do the Americans and EU support, both here in our homeland and in Ukraine? We had no choice but to send troops into Crimea. People like Aleksander Muzychku were killed like dogs in the street. But we have to ask ourselves whose interests are really being served when people like us, people who share the same ancestry and same territory, shed each other's blood?'

'Yes', Sveta agreed. 'Lviv declared independence for Ukraine whilst 15,000 rallied under the Russian flag in Simferopol. I think Svoboda and Pravy Sektor are being funded by Judaic interests. Poroshenko, the chocolate magnate, is one of the Chosen. So is Yulia Tymoshenko. She urged the "wiping out of all the *katsaps*."' Tom looked unsure. 'It is a bad name the Ukrainians have for Russians', she explained. 'There is talk once again of child ritual murders in Kiev, like the Youshchinsky case back in 1911.'

'Look, we still have people like Igor Strelkov supporting Alexander Bordai and Igor Plotnitsky in Lugansk', Alexander insisted. Then for Tom's benefit, he added, 'Strelkov's the centurion who took the executive building in Sloviansk with the tacit support of the Defence Minister, Sergei Shoygu.'

'Isn't Strelkov former SBU?' asked Tom. No one seemed sure.

'Some say he goes by the alias Girkin, too.' Sveta shrugged.

'But his open call for support from the Kremlin didn't get universal support, certainly not from Sergey Kurginyan of the All Russian Patriotic Movement, or even that GRU crony Vladislav Surkov', Tom said, nonplussed.

'That was a mistake we will live to regret', acknowledged Grigori. 'But the grey cardinal doesn't play all his cards at once. And anyway, the Duginites are concerned that the architect of managed democracy, as we call him, is really an Israeli agent.'

'Our people in Donetsk are the vanguard for No-vorossiya!' Alexander blurted. 'I liked what Zakha-renchenko said about the Jew pencilnecks. "I can't re-member a time when Cossacks were led by people who had never held a sword in their hands."'

'They've even got women's fighting units in the peo-ple's militia', Sveta added.

'That bastard Kolomoisky gave the order for the shoot-ings in Odessa, but all we hear is whining from that Chief Rabbi Azman!' Dimitry was less than impressed. 'And that Zionist front-man, Petro Poroshenko, is still calling for total war with Russia!'

'There was a time when Putin claimed Russia could take Kiev in two weeks', Tom contributed.

'With what result, more Slav deaths? More mourning mothers crying over sealed coffins in Ussurikysk? Hun-dreds of thousands of our people fleeing to camps in bor-der areas like Sumy?' said Alexander.

'The EU has special forces in western Ukraine operat-ing under cover of a no-fly zone, and we have civil strife in the East. It is just like the partition of Cyprus', Dimitry postulated. Grigori looked on.

'And the Jews are working to control the oil and gas deposits in the Mediterranean Sea, also!'

- ❖ Following the installation of NATO's Missile De-fence Shield, President Babel signs a new strategic arms agreement with the UN, NATO, and the EU confirming Russia's compliance with the non-use of strategic weapons to resolve current geopolitical disputes. Teams of UN inspectors arrive at various missile launch sites to monitor the situation;
- ❖ Pro-Putin deputies in the Duma speak to a large crowd gathered in Manege Square calling for the former President's return to office;
- ❖ State media show Prime Minister Viktor Akulov lighting candles at the funeral for those killed in Ufa;

- ❖ The Russian 31ˢᵗ Separate Airborne Assault Brigade are flown in to Leonidovka from their home base in Ulyanovsk to secure chemical weapon stores;
- ❖ UN peacekeeping forces cross the Polish-Ukrainian border at Eava-Ruska and Ustrzyki-Dolne;
- ❖ The Muslim Federation's offer to provide troops as part of the peacekeeping arrangements in Ukraine is warmly welcomed by the EU;
- ❖ Joint EU and Muslim forces operating west of the Dnieper stop their advance 50 kilometres from Kiev;
- ❖ EU leaders interrupt emergency meetings with the Russian delegation in Strasbourg about the best way to respond to the 'Great Migration' humanitarian crisis in order to face Jerusalem during their prayers;
- ❖ UN armoured columns comprising personnel carriers, and Leclerc and Polish PT-91 tanks supported by F-4E aircraft operating out of the Holzdorf Airbase enter Lutsk, Rivne, and Lviv;
- ❖ The encirclement of Ivano-Frankovsk results in mass arrests of extremists and allegations of mistreatment of deportees in the hastily established containment centres near Lublin and Zamosc;
- ❖ Rumours of mass drownings in Lake Hancza are steadfastly denied by sources in Brussels and Warsaw;
- ❖ The Royal Navy enters the Black Sea in a deliberate act of provocation against the Russian fleet based in Sevastopol.

'What do you think the wars in Syria and the threats to Iran are all about?' Grigori barked. 'Americans scream about human rights but still support anti-Assad rebels who eat the hearts of their enemies. They fund groups like ISIS and see the world through a distorted lens. Some of our own worst gangsters have been welcomed to Western countries with open arms, and we have created scapegoats at home who our enemies champion as martyrs. Think of the journalists who have died mysteriously, the frauds like Khordokovsky and Berezovsky. They robbed Russia once and their type will try again.'

'Things were different before, the old President got control over the oligarchs', Dimitry asserted.

'Or was their partner?' Sveta echoed. 'Putin was a functionary of the *sistema*. Who passed the law criminalising anyone challenging the findings of the Nuremberg trials? Who talked about the threat of militant nationalism? Both Fradkov and Chubais wear the Star of David. Lavrov went around Europe making speeches about the rise of anti-Semitism. I think he was a Fifth Columnist.'

'We need someone like Alexander Lukashenko or Islam Karimov', Dimitry demanded.

'Head boilers!' Sveta interjected. 'Better, our old friend from *Zavtra*, Alexander Prokhanov, Zakhar Prilepin, and Konstantin Malofeev at the Valaam monastery.'

'Yes, and also people like Baron Ungern-Sternberg, Captain Semenov, and Mikhail Drozdovsky, who liberated Rostov from the Red Army', Tom chimed in wistfully.

'I want a Zil-4112P to drive me around', Alexander toasted drunkenly.

'And an Ilyushin jet with a solid gold toilet to shit in!' screeched Grigori.

An hour later, they were still drinking. Anger was still evident when they recalled the riots in Sokolniki Park and the killing of a Spartak football fan, Egor Sviridov, by 'them'. Then there was that Cameroonian 'artist' Pierre Narcisse, who had married a blonde Russian. Another O J Simpson slaying in the making. They agreed that it had been a positive sign that Putin had broached the subject of declining White demographics, but nothing had been done. The anti-immigrant riots in Kanopoga in Karelia in 2006, the fighting in Manezhnaya Square in downtown Moscow in 2010, and the rocketing crime statistics had all been ignored. Azeri, Chechen, and Georgian gangs dealt in arms, drugs, prostitutes, and scrap metal. The 3000 or so poppy fields in Uzbekistan and the infinite cannabis production of Kazakhstan had fuelled their takeover of the underworld from St Petersburg to Vladivostok. There were whispered expressions like *inorodnye, khokhol,* and *ishak.* Then there were references to *sobornost* and *solidarism,* the Harbin Russian Club, Konstantin Rodzaevsky, the ideologue Mikhail Mikhailovich Grott, Vasilyev's *Pamyat,* Barkashov's street fighters, Red-Brown alliances, Rutskoy, and the October 1993 rising. Soon they were raising glasses again, this time to the long-dead heroes of the 'Hundred'. Then the New Generationists, people like Menshikov, Ustrialov, and Tikhomirov. They finished by honouring the exile Anastase Vonsiatsky and Danilevsky's notion of a Slavic mission to save the world.

'I have an original copy of *Vehki!*' Dimitry announced.

'Ah', said Grigori, 'so much for Berdyaev's words . . . a conservative man of letters today is almost a contradiction in terms . . . '

'I hear the same comments from current American pundits', said Tom.

'Same dirty tactic to marginalise us', Grigori said. 'You know our security services told the FBI about the Boston bomber, Tamerlan Tsanaev.' Tom recognised the words Chechen and terrorist as they punctured the rapid Russian dialogue like bullets with a displaced centre of gravity, the ones that spiral through human flesh, lodging in the most difficult places in the bones for a surgeon to get at. 'We can't even protect the children in our schools or the people going out to the theatre', Grigori cursed. 'I tell you, Beslan shamed us. The Shahidkas set off bombs in our train stations and on our trolley buses.' Tom recalled hearing of the thirty or so dead in Volgograd and seeing the uncensored TV footage of the Russian officer crucified in the city square in Grozny years before. The brutal execution of Rodionov, a young conscript clinging to his silver cross, even as his killer, Khaikhoroyev, sawed at his throat with a rusty blade, still haunted his mind. 'And all this in the name of the desert god, Mohammed. Our armies have not been destroyed in battle', Grigori was preaching. 'Both Napoleon and Hitler were stopped in Russia. Our retreat from East Germany was a terrible mistake. Between 1989 and 1991 we gave up an empire. Armenia, Belarus, Estonia, Azerbaijan, Georgia, Kazakhstan, Kyrgyzstan, Latvia, Lithuania, Moldova, Tajikistan, Turkmenistan, Ukraine, and Uzbekistan. At least our intervention in Crimea and South Ossetia arrested that decline!'

'Back then our confidence was gone', Dimitry moaned, 'Remember Unit 20004? The officers stole the soldier's wages. I blame the General Staff!'

'No', Sveta said. 'It was Gorbachev's mistake not to join the August Coup.'

'Better they had seized Yeltsin and kept him in Zavidovo.' Grigori sounded morose, even bitter.

'Don't talk to me of that hero', someone breathed like hot steam. 'What a fool, standing on top of that tank and shaking his fist. It is a pity one of those Alpha sharpshooters did not put him out of his misery.'

'Like they did with Boris Nemtsov?'

'California style!'

'Put us all out of our misery', they laughed, raising glasses in salute.

'But at least it meant the end of a one-party state', ventured Tom tentatively.

'You think?' Grigori's drunken face betrayed his ill-temper. 'Listen, English', he said, 'the government bombed our own people in Ryazan with hexogen to cause a backlash against the Chechens just to keep themselves in power. The Americans learned that trick from us. But as always, they had to do it in a bigger way. Look at the *USS Liberty* incident. That was a false flag attack! What do you think the Twin Towers were?

'Well, I don't know. Are you a 911 conspiracy theorist?'

'Well, George Orwell is one of you, no?'

'One of what?'

'British writer!'

'Yes, so?'

'Think about *Nineteen Eighty-Four*.'

'What about it?'

'Well, Osama bin Laden was Goldstein. You think Big Brother is just a stupid TV show on BBC?'

'Well . . . '

'No, you'll see that it is true.' He swilled yet more alcohol. 'The one-party state is all over the world now. Globalism is paramount. That is why people like Dugin are hunted down. It is written in the Eurasian Mission Statement that "we Eurasianists defend on principle the necessity to preserve the existence of every people on earth, the blossoming variety of cultures and religious traditions, the unquestionable right of the peoples to independently choose their own path of historical development". Is there a difference between the Democrats and Republicans in Washington? I cannot see any. Is there a real divide between Labour or Conservatives in Westminster? I think not.'

'But *The Sunday Times* is not *Pravda*, yet!'

'You say not. I say, yes!' Grigori slapped his guest on the shoulder. 'Alexander Temerko, a man who made billions out of the Yukos fraud, funds your Conservative Party. Fukuyama's *Open Society* translates into whole populations coming under the control of those same people who run the world of finance and have a monopoly on the world's media. We are all being assimilated into a One World Government.'

'So Eurasianists think that by forming a Berlin, Moscow, and New Dehli axis they can counter the forces of Western Atlanticism?'

'Leonid Savin said, "Russia is not part of Europe or Asia" . . . we will oppose Neo-Liberalism to our dying breath.'

'I'm guessing you are not a big fan of Francis Fukuyama's *The End of History*, then.'

'Hell, no!'

'Anyway, I think his influence over American foreign policy is long gone.'

'Yes, now he talks of state-building.' Grigori could barely hide his distaste. 'Listen, my friend, who was Saddam
Hussein's biggest supporter in the war with Iran? Who
invaded Iraq and why? What did your Tony Blair stand to
gain? Who was pulling his strings? Same question now
with Assad's last stand in Aleppo and Damascus. We
stood our ground alongside General Mohammad Ali Jafa-
ri's Iranian Revolutionary Guard, who came to defend
Sharyat and Tiyas against those IS fanatics. But who funds
them and who pulls America's strings?' Fat fingers played
the puppeteer with invisible puppets over the table.

'I'm too drunk to debate', Tom protested. Grigori
poured him another.

'Not drunk enough!' he shouted. 'We were in Afghanistan, remember. We saw this *jihad* at close quarters long
before your people ever did.'

Around midnight, a black BMW came to collect him,
its bumper rubbing tight-up to the blockwork, headlights
blinking twice as a signal for Tom to leave. All along the
Griboedova embankment, people were leaning, comatose,
on the iron-work, languorously smoking cigarettes, bottles
of Danish beer lined up one after another along the cold
stone wall. In the Sakura, a passing waitress helped Tom
to find his coat. Saying goodnight, he stepped outside, his
breath forming a lattice scarf of French needle-point before him.

Walking around to the back of the car, Tom pulled on
the door handle, reassured by the click of German engi-
neering.

'Would you like a tour of the city by night?' asked the
silver-haired driver as Professor Hunter sank into the deep
leather seat.

'Why not?' He felt happy, succumbing to the eddy
cocktail of alcohol and jet lag. His arms stretched out
across the spacious cream interior, smelling of leather
polish and jasmine air freshener. Suddenly, the car
jumped the kerb. There was a cat's squeal of burning rub-

ber as the vehicle spun along a tight spiral arc. Tom caught a glimpse of the driver smiling mischievously in the rear-view mirror.

'I will show you a good time', he promised. There was a curl to his lip like a wild dog let off the leash. Pedestrians scattered to left and right in the rogue's headlights. Tom gripped the door handle as the car shot along the waterside, weaving between oncoming traffic, out past the mosaic domes of the old Cathedral and the Mikhaylovskiy Gardens. They rushed across narrow bridges, under the outstretched metal arms of 1930s street lighting. They emerged onto a stretch of road between the old city and the brooding Neva.

'This is a good place to walk in daytime.' Tom noted the ominous emphasis on daytime. To his right he could see the city spread-eagled across the smoky blue horizon. His tired eyes drifted over the bridges to the shimmering windows running along Kamennoostrovsky Prospekt.

'Over there is Petrograd and Vasilievsky', said the driver. 'You can visit the battle ship *Aurora*. Do you know the history of the Revolution?' For a moment the Professor's memory was filled with shaky old black-and-white newsreels of a crowd surging up against a thin line of troops, plumes of gun smoke, Comrade Lenin standing on a banner-strewn platform, clenched fist pumping.

'I know a little', he replied, rightfully reckoning his guide had lived through the Brezhnev epoch and been dumbfounded by the Gorbachev turnabout. He thought it best not to raise difficult subjects and just to let sleeping dogs lie.

'This side', the man continued like a well-rehearsed tour guide, 'is the Marble Palace, built by Rinaldi in 1768. It was a gift for Catherine the Great's right-hand man, Orlov. Now it is an art gallery. I have been there many times. If you like eighteenth-century paintings, then this is a good place for you.'

They drove on. 'Now this is spectacular, the Hermitage, one of the biggest museums in the world. There are artefacts from Egypt, India, and China. My favourite place is the gallery where they keep works by Leonardo da Vinci, Titian, Raphael, Matisse, and Michelangelo. Very big exhibit, you must give yourself time.'

Fifty metres ahead, the traffic lights were rolling to red. The driver cursed loudly, flicked his headlights on and off to warn of his intentions, then floored the accelerator onto Dvortsovvy Proezd. To the left was a vast circle of buildings and a flat square with a massive stone column rising like a strong muscular arm out of the ground. Tom thought it seemed to be reaching greedily upwards to grab for the Moon.

'The Alexander column took four years to build. It is made from Karelian granite. The idea was to celebrate Imperial Russia's victory over Napoleon.' For a second, the Professor tried to recall how the little Corsican Emperor had marched in ahead of half a million men and crawled out with less than twenty thousand. 'I came here with thousands of other people to light a candle for Zhirinovsky. My wife did not agree, but I came all the same. You know, before he was assassinated, he said, "Russia once saved the world from the Ottoman Empire by sending its troops to the south. Seven centuries ago we stopped the Mongols. We have saved Europe several times: from the south, from the East, from the north and from the centre of Europe itself. The world should be grateful to Russia for its role as saviour." He was a great man . . .' His voice broke off in the dark, his pain palpable, almost as if he was reliving the day when the leader of the Liberal Democratic Party of Russia was gunned down in the street. 'A great, great man . . .'

The whole square was filled with a mournful blue tint. One could imagine the Imperial troops parading before their Tsar, starched epaulettes and sabres shining in thin northern light. 'Most of the buildings were designed by Rastrelli in the Baroque style. They are large, no?' Tom nodded silently, overwhelmed by the endless contours of pink and yellow facades as they undulated, curving away

in symmetrical lines off the square. To his right, the trees
of the Admiralty Gardens stood tall against the buildings,
twisting trunks casting fluttering silhouettes beyond the
skein of encroaching streetlights that shone like pale
torches through green-lime leaves.

They circled the gardens slowly. Tom made out vam-
piric shapes wandering about under the tree cover. Then,
without warning, the BMW pulled over onto leaf-strewn
Admiralteyskiy Proezd. He heard the driver open the front
door and watched as he got out and walked away from the
car. For a moment, the Professor became anxious. Beads
of sweat broke out on his forehead. Was he being set up?
Then the footsteps stopped and he saw a cigarette light
up. The car doors on either side swung open. Tom looked
quickly to his left and right as two girls, one blonde and
one brunette, slid across smooth leather. Before he knew
what was happening he felt two thin arms wrap around
his neck, a hot tongue invade his mouth, and a second
pair of eager hands unzip his trousers.

Back in his hotel room, Tom waited a few moments before switching on the light. He was looking down onto the
traffic below. The girls stood behind in the shadows, unsure what to expect: tears or passion? Most men could not
wait to tear into their flesh, but there were some who
snivelled on endlessly about their broken hearts and sad
lives. They sensed this client was very different. He was
cool and detached, thoughtful and reckless all at the same
time. After a while, he went to the minibar and poured
them two flutes of champagne and a large tumbler of
whisky for himself. He stood looking up at the Cathedral
through the huge window, sipping at his scotch, thinking
hard, his black jacket cast carelessly over a chair.

They watched him closely, studying his long, slim body
set against the illuminated dome. A ballet of stars danced
on tip-toe over the frosted cupola. Below, the last trailing
troop of revellers were making their way home. They
thought his room, all cream-coloured duvets and red

headboards, was just like a film set. And they liked making that kind of film. The girls began slipping out of their clothes, pale shoulders and slim-finned swimmer's hips reflecting in the luminous mirror. One drew an ice cube over her breasts in order to entice him. The other was spooning ice cream from the minibar.

The door to the drinks cabinet was hanging open, almost leering, showing off miniature bottles of vodka and gin. He swirled his glass, listening to chunks of ice clink against crystal. His eyes fixed on the perfect bodies disrobing before him. He felt surprisingly reinvigorated considering that he had been on a non-stop lecturing tour for weeks on end. London to San Francisco, then Vancouver and Quebec. Returning to London temporarily, he had flown on to Bratislava, and now the Baltic. It had become a blur of airport lounges, tubular steel, and tinted perspex. He had been strip-searched and questioned about his baggage and the purpose of his journey by uniformed officials of every colour, height, weight, and sexual orientation.

'I'm Anna', the blonde breathed as a beautifully manicured hand tousled his hair. He felt a tongue flick wetly over his stiffening nipples. Simultaneously, pointed breasts pressed into his back.

'And I'm Oksana . . .' Arms surrounded him, warm palms caressing his buttocks. He found their voices irresistible as they chattered to each other, occasionally breaking into English, telling him what they were going to do to him, h ow they would make him feel. After a few moments they had removed his shirt and trousers. His watch read 02.15. Their three bodies were framed by the window. The street outside was quiet now, only the night wind walked the pavements and courtyards. Whirling chocolate wrappers darted about the square, scratching pale stone, colliding with railings, catching in the prickling branches stretched out before the vast doors of St Isaac's Cathedral. There, all alone, a couple stood bathed in wet moonlight. They were talking intently, hands gesturing before they walked on, casting ghostly shadows under the streetlight in the far corner of the square. Her long brown hair flowed over his shoulder.

Tom let the curtain fall on the scene, finished his whisky, and dropped onto the bed beside his two companions. He began to take his pleasure mechanically, gratified by the wet sensations he was feeling and the sucking sounds that filled his ears. His eyes drifted over the room one last time before he switched off the bedside light. His briefcase was open on the table. The laptop's screen threw a metallic stare at the far wall. Mouths and fingers roamed. The scent of musky orifices filled his nostrils as they all worked towards a simultaneous spasm. Afterwards, slowly but surely, they relaxed into an uneasy sleep, Anna's head on his chest and Oksana's bony knee jutting his kidney.

He woke with a telephone ringing near his ear. A thin digital pulse cut the dead black air. Fumbling for the bedside lamp, Tom eventually found the light switch. A woman's arm lolled over his thigh. His eyes squinted at the alarm clock. It was 03.20. He picked up the receiver.

'Hello', he rasped.

'This is reception', a woman replied. 'I have a call for you.'

'Are you sure?'

'Yes, I am sure.'

'I'm not expecting a call.'

'They insist, sir!'

'Ok, put them through', Tom grumbled, dry-mouthed, failing to mask his frustration.

'Hello', came Grigori's voice down a crackling line. 'Did you enjoy my little entertainment?'

'Entertainment?'

'The girls?'

'Yes, but how . . .'

'I arranged with the driver in advance . . .'

'Well, they are very beautiful . . .' he went on awkwardly.

'And friendly, no?'

'Decidedly!'

'They are recommended. I wanted to make sure . . .'

'I'm grateful but also very tired', Tom hinted.

'I understand you very well, English', Grigori guffawed. 'Listen, I need you to go to the Peter and Paul Fortress tomorrow morning. You will meet one of my people in the tomb of the Tsars.'

'Who?' the Professor asked. 'How will I know him?'

'It is a woman, Iryna. She will find you. Go there at ten.' The phone went dead. Tom cradled the receiver and rolled over on the pillow. A face shrouded in blonde hair emerged from the sheets to greet his lips. He heard the sound of a cellophane condom wrap popping.

'Fuck?' she asked.

2.

Stand thou, O Peter's citadel, like Russia steadfast
and enduring . . .—Pushkin

The city centre was bathed in storm-blue light. Radiating
streets of equidistant nineteenth-century mansions were
reflected in dull water. Stern terraces stretched away in
austere straight lines as far as the eye could see.

Tom stepped off the kerb, joining the pedestrians moving cautiously to avoid a line of belching Lada taxis circling the square. To his right, the Cathedral dome was
shrouded in cloud; to his left was the overbearing classi-
cism of the Mariinsky Palace. He was pressed by people in
long winter coats, jaws set hard against frosty daylight,
resenting the imposition of the wage slave culture on the
former proletarian people's utopia.

Stopping for a moment, he watched bandy-legged Asi-
atics in skin-tight Levis point their cameras at the tower-
ing bronze of Nicholas the First, balancing uncomfortably
on his galloping steed. The Emperor's metallic form was
slowly disappearing behind the haze falling across the façade of the St Petersburg City Council building.

The Professor's eyes were drawn to the national flag
tugging defiantly in a Baltic breeze. How different from
1917, when an armoured car flying a red pennant stood
with its gun trained on St Isaac's and revolutionary guards
wielded bolt-action carbines behind makeshift barricades.
The murder and savagery of those days was still etched in
the streets. Nobody was immune, no family escaped a visit
to the lime pit.

Walking under sparse trees, along yellow gravel paths
forming trails beyond the great columned hulk of the Ca-

thedral, he could see the sturdy haunches of the Bronze Horseman galloping towards the oily Bolshaya Neva. The river cut like a roiling charcoal snake between the Admiralty and the University embankments. Tom lingered, staring at the powerful figure set against the steely skyline. The sculptor had spent hours drawing horses in motion before the casting. There was, he thought, a certain irony that this very embodiment of speed and action should be so firmly embedded in solid stone. Yet another one of those contradictions that punctuated his walk along the riverside, where young drunks fell about in alcohol-induced stupors, whilst old men played chess or fished quietly from steps that descended in great waxen slabs to the water's edge.

Across the river, the palaces, porcelain blue and egg-shell yellow, were being bombarded by streaks of bitter citrus sunlight. The spire of the Peter and Paul fortress was a golden spear, pointing far into the sky beyond the Dvortsovy Most Bridge. He crossed over the Neva with the gargantuan Hermitage Museum looming over his hunched shoulders. Blind windows stared vacantly outward, following his every move. Inside, gigantic rooms filled with amber, gold, and emeralds gathered dust. Endless corridors were stacked with spectacular artwork. Now Tom's imagination was racing. He was simultaneously scared and excited to see more and more of this fairy tale of obelisks and gemstones, with all its fading grandeur and glistening steeples.

The sea wind picked up when he was midway over the bridge. A passenger ferry passed below, its engine pumping, wafts of burnt diesel pushing up through the blackened metal grating at his feet. Commuters swung briefcases and handbags. He was caught in a maelstrom of flapping ties and flailing scarves. Ahead, he could see a crowd of protesters gathering under the huge phallic columns of the Strelka Vasilevskogo.

Tom let the office workers pass, watching a gap-toothed Nikita Khrushchev lookalike pitch his stall at the

base of one of the big rostral columns. The erstwhile
tradesman was wearing a shabby army coat and a woollen
hat with hammer-and-sickle insignia. The Professor
doubted he was a genuine veteran. Stubby, fat fingers
tumbled dice. Rouble notes were exchanged across a
weather-beaten table. Looking over his left shoulder, back
towards the north bank, he caught sight of a huge bear
pacing along the wide parapet above the river. A coiled
chain dragged uneasily along the ground behind. It stood
on stout hind legs, pawing the sky, its dull fur coat matted
with a crust of dirt. It had staring onyx eyes, bayonet claws
spreading out before its snorting snout.

Tom strolled over the Birzhevoy Most Bridge to the
Petrograd side. He pushed against a stream of students
rushing to the State University, their lecture rooms clus-
tered in a honeycomb of antique architecture around the
Menshikov Palace. Bright, happy faces were wrapped in
coloured scarves, bags on shoulders, tossing butts in gut-
ters, splashing through puddles in front of the Pushkin
House. They stood in groups, passing iPods or magazines.
Some single ones sat on a wall, legs dangling loosely, cat-
calling their friends, laughing and jeering. It was a snap-
shot of European and American cities from the 1950s and
'60s: a homogenous demographic with no compromises to
the pretence of multicultural chic. Inspired, the Englishman recalled Francis Parker Yockey's idea that Bolshevism, once free of the Zionist yoke, could be used as a lev-
er against Pan-Slavic nationalism. He promised to himself
that he would re-read the philosopher's *The World in
Flames* the minute he returned home.

Moving on, he could see the walls of the Peter and Paul
fortress in the distance, the edifice scrabbling like a lob-
ster, labouring under the weight of its own shell down to
the sandy river bank. It struck him as a sinister presence
in the centre of Rastrelli's neo-classical wedding cake. It
was an impenetrable, unfathomable, and infamous geo-
metrical maze at the heart of the city. Its dark vaults were
home to the ghosts of generations of revolutionaries who

had been hung on meat-hooks for their beliefs.

Crossing the ancient St John's Bridge under St Peter's Gate, where a two-headed eagle and a horseman slaying a dragon motif stood proud, he entered into the cold, hard belly of the place. To right and left, carvings of Bellona, goddess of war, and Minerva, goddess of wisdom, confronted him. Directly in front stood the Cathedral, with its vast spire pointing at the gathering clouds. Tom walked in the shadow of Trezzini's Tower. The wind whipped the walls, rising and falling like a condemned man's death rattle. The smell of the river was in his nostrils, a fetid infusion of oil on metal. He could almost see the spectral memories of ill-fated dissidents flicker and curve through the grey veil circling about the golden angel one hundred twenty metres above the citadel. The sound of shuffling feet and a sense of awed rapture greeted him as he pushed on a carved wooden door and stepped inside.

It was a magnificent diamante ballroom, covered with iconostasis. Entombed bones in white sarcophagi lay under gold crosses. Small groups of people wandered about, hands clutching guidebooks, eyes lifted toward the artworks. All the Russian emperors had been buried here before the Revolution, their tombs made of Altai jasper and hand-polished rodonite from the distant Ural Mountains. Side galleries were filled with the crypts of princes and royal relatives.

He looked around, hoping to catch someone's eye. There were no clues in the faces of the people he met who were circling the paintings. In a small room, close to Peter and Catherine's marble colonnade, where the last of the Romanovs had finally been laid to rest, a tall, thin woman with thick black hair stepped forward and asked his name.

'Tom Hunter.'

'I'm Iryna.' She extended a hand. 'Grigori informs me that you would like a guided tour of the citadel.'

'Yes, very much', he answered.

'That is good.' Then, with an expansive gesture, she started. 'In here are the coffins of Nicholas, Alexander, and their murdered children. Not all of them are accounted for, which gives rise to legends that Anastasia survived the killings in Ekaterinburg.'

'What do you think happened?'

'I think she was raped and murdered like her sisters, but they have not yet found the body.'

'No chance she was smuggled out of the country and her descendants are living in New York, then?'

'They shot them, stabbed them with bayonets, and then burnt them.'

'Makes a good story, though.'

'So does the Loch Ness monster!'

Outside, they walked in the footsteps of hundreds of prisoners. Lichen-covered block fell away into rippling rollers that rushed to lick the feet of the fortress. Above, a smudged Sun reflected off the tall, arched windows cut deep into the high parapet.

'Originally, the city was to be a naval base and trading centre. Peter the Great had been to Holland and wanted to match the Europeans for military and merchant power. The architecture is English, Italian, French, and Dutch. There is very little Russian style. It was a new beginning. Moscow and Slav fashions were not accepted. Noblemen were told to make their palaces here. There was a decree that nowhere else could build in stone. All the stonemak-ers . . .' She hesitated.

'Stonemasons', Tom prompted. Iryna raised a smile at his gentle correction.

' . . . stonemasons, came to St Petersburg. The city was planned out like Amsterdam and Venice, geometric and rectilinear. It had been this way in Europe since the Re-naissance, but not in the East, which was still twisted and medieval.'

'And the population in more recent times?'

'I think one million by the late nineteenth century, and two million by the time of the Revolution.'

'Much smaller than London.'

'London', she radiated. 'I would love to see Buckingham Palace. You know, I always watch the BBC to see the new baby come home from hospital with Catherine and William?' The wind picked up, Tom shuddered, and Iryna returned to her narrative. 'They say that in the first years, the workforce in Peter's city lost one hundred and fifty thousand lives to disease and exhaustion. Soon they had to bring labourers in from elsewhere to raise the houses. Two to one, or four to one ratios of street width to building height were used to provide balance to the rooftops. There was to be harmony in every design.'

'Sounds so perfect!'

'Perfect, no! The Russians were peasant people, close to the land and their animals', Iryna insisted. 'Like Lobanov once said, "a nation moved to a city is doomed to extinction". Peter was trying to make us European before our time!'

'It seems that in every age there has been an idea that has cost thousands of lives.'

'We know all about those ideas here. Ideologies come in sachets with breakfast cereals.' They walked in silence for a few minutes before Tom asked why she was involved in politics. 'Because I like the music of Alexander Galich, who sang "Petersburg Romance"':

Our era is testing us.
Can you go out in the square?
Do you dare go out on the square
At the agreed time?

'It was a song about the defiance of the Decembrists, performed in May 2012 in front of St Isaacs.'

'And the underground here, is it strong?'

'There's some splinter groups from Sergey Kurginan's Young Guard against Orangism, and Vladimir Yermolaev's Movement Against Illegal Immigration.'

'Wasn't the immigration movement banned and Yermolaev detained?'

'During the so-called Snow-Revolution, yes. But revolutionary movements grow here like a virus. The Great Mosque', her finger pointing over the Neva, 'is a call to arms. Ever since the times of Pushkin and Turgenev, the city has been ripe for insurrection. Now there is also Krylov's Russian Social Movement and Oreshkin's Union of Right Forces.'

'And the objectives of the movement you are involved with?'

'To return Russia to the Russians.'

'A worthy goal.'

'Our aims have been generally consistent since the Society of St Cyril and St Methodius and Ivan Kireyevsky's Society of Wisdom Lovers, Lyubomurdy, to foment *Pravoslavyni*, Orthodox patriotism, and to strengthen national self-consciousness, *natsionalnoe samosznanie*. I agree with Vladimir Skvortsov that the clergy are a dependable force with "deeply national and patriotic commitments representing supremacy in the face of the rootless and cosmopolitan intelligentsia". Even many of the early Decembrist leaders who were imprisoned here, people like Pavel Pestel, held very strong nationalist views. Some of our historians, like Nikolai Knedamzin, argued then that every Russian should have a piece of land, even if that was at the price of serfdom, military dictatorship, or the sacrifice of human rights.'

Tom's face balked at the idea. Iryna shrugged.

'Personal freedoms do not feed your babies.'

'Yes, but . . .'

'Russia has always strived to develop a fundamentally non-European state structure, a fusion of Slavic autocracy and Western democracy.'

'A difficult task?'

'Almost impossible, as our history attests, but it has not stopped us trying!'

❖ Thousands of anti-austerity protestors take to the streets of St Petersburg and Moscow, clashing with

Omon units on the Lomonsov bridge over the Neva and the Great Moskvoretsky Bridge, in full view of St Basil's Cathedral;

❖ Russian National Unity paramilitaries begin to organise in response to President Babel's declaration that 'fascist reactionaries will play no part in Russia's multicultural future';

❖ Several negro, gay, and trans people are found dead in the back streets of Moscow's Vnukkovo district following an assault on a local schoolgirl;

❖ Citizens' food distribution centres open up all over the country. Those in Tverskaya Ulitsa in Moscow, Bolshaia Pokrovskaia in Nizhny Novgorod, and the Kalininsky District of St Petersburg are immediately surrounded and shut down by armed militia operating under direct orders from the Kremlin;

❖ Alexei Navalny and his brother Oleg, both with a string of convictions for defrauding the French cosmetic company Yves Rocher, distance themselves from earlier statements made during interviews with *Russia Today* where they had reminded people of their activism in the 'Stop Feeding the Caucasus' campaign, and described dark-skinned Caucasian immigrants as cockroaches. 'Cockroaches can be killed with a slipper; as for humans, I recommend a pistol';

❖ Yulia Navalny is interviewed about her fears for her husband, a man identified as one of the top hundred most influential thinkers by *Time Magazine* back in 2012. 'He is under threat from Nazis!' she claimed;

❖ A mayor of a small provincial town is arrested for quoting Bulgakov in reference to *vnenarodnost*, the alien character of the intelligentsia, along with cryptic allusions as to who was responsible for the mass famine of 1921;

❖ 'For God's sake', demands a historian accused of writing anti-Semitic articles, 'even Putin openly stated that 85 percent of the Bolshevik leaders were Jews';

❖ Utro Rossii (Dawn of Russia) patriots begin talking openly about *Novus Ordo Seclorum*, the total population manipulation and resource extraction enacted by a One World Government masked under talk of Liberty and Equality.

'Essentially, Russia has historically had three options. Slow absorption into Europe, as Krizhanich or Golitsyn wanted. Isolationism, as preached by Ioakhim. Or forced modernisation, like Peter the Great and Stalin tried. But in more recent times there was the relatively large and often overlooked anti-Marxist and pro-Christian underground that was dedicated to overthrowing the Communist state. This was something my grandparents and parents participated in. Their programme included statements like, "The life and dignity of the person are inviolable; all citizens are equal before the law; the freedom of labour is provided for everyone by the right of each citizen to land and to credit; all methods of dissemination of thought are free; gatherings and demonstrations are free and the secret political police must be disbanded".'

'Sounds very reasonable.'

'Their plan was to start a military coup and establish a theocratic state!'

'I get nervous when people bring God into politics!'

Iryna nodded. 'But God can be a radical force. St Michael the Archangel said, "Towards the unholy hearts who seek entrance into the most Holy House of the Lord with no mercy I point my sword".'

'And who in your opinion are the Unholy?'

'Christ was sent to the world and not to the Jewish people alone. What was the first thing the Bolsheviks attacked? Tradition in the form of religion. In the Kremlin alone they destroyed the Church of Our Saviour near the Terem Palaces, the Church of Konstantin and Elena, the Church of Annunciation in the Rye Yard, then the two chapels at the Spassky Gates and the Church of the Nativity of John the Baptist. You are no doubt familiar with Filofei's theory, "*Dva Rima padosha, a tretii, a chetvertom ne byti*"?'

'That two Romes have fallen, Moscow is third and a fourth will never be!'

'The Bishop's Council that met in Moscow in 2013 declared, "Orthodoxy is being reborn as the foundation of national self-consciousness, uniting all the healthy forces in society—those forces which strive for the transformation of life on the basis of a sure foundation and the spiritual and moral values that have entered the flesh and blood of our peoples".'

'But still, so much for prophets, I say.'

'Indeed, but we need a strong Orthodox Church now. Otherwise the Muslims will overrun us. In Dostoevsky's *Brothers Karamazov*, there is a line predicting our regenerative qualities: "A star shall rise in the east".'

'God aside, your writers are seers!' he complimented her.

'Not all. Lev Tolstoy participated in the destruction of the national faith.'

'And for Dostoevsky, "A people without nationality is like a man without a personality".'

'It is true, Dostoevsky became highly conservative in his later years. He believed Russia carried a divine candle to light the darkness of this world.'

'And are those beliefs still prevalent?'

'Among some on the nationalist Right, yes!'

'Such messianic fervour can lead to madness!'

'To have no sense of mission is worse. Of course there are many who are simply touched by the aesthetic of what Leontiev calls "the beards, pussy-willows, icons, poetry of prayer and fasting". But thinkers like Theodosius of the Caves and Kirill of the White Lake thought nationality a holy ideal. Berdyaev suggests that through faith we could stop "the exploitation of man by man, as well as the exploitation of man by the state", which for him was the way

our economic elites converted man *into an object*. Solzhenitsyn was the same.' Iryna stopped to quote him. '"I think
Russia, which has thrown open the gates of Hell in the
world, is alone capable of trying to close them . . . there
are in the West no hands of such strength and no heart of
such wisdom . . . either the world will soon perish or the
hands to defeat hell will come from the enslaved East".'

'And Tolstoy said, everyone thinks of changing the
world, but no one thinks of changing himself.'

'Touché!'

* ❖ OPEC reduces the cost of a barrel of oil to $28;
* ❖ The Federal Bank's life-long President, Janet Yellen,
  raises US interest rates for the third quarter in succession on advice from consultants operating out of
  Tel Aviv;
* ❖ Otkritie Bank officials close foreign exchange coun-
  ters after a 300 percent increase in demand for Eu-
  ros;
* ❖ Fighting is reported outside a branch of Sberbank
  opposite Kursky station in Central Moscow when
  people are turned away by private security guards;
* ❖ Russia reassesses its GDP forecasts downwards by
  23 percent over the previous quarter;
* ❖ Rosneft, the state-owned oil company, is declared
  bankrupt, having failed to service the substantial
  foreign debt it incurred in order to buy out TNK-
  BP;
* ❖ Superstitious belief is reinvigorated by unexplained
  thunderclaps across the skies of western Russia;
* ❖ Talk of EU and American stealth weapons becomes
  common.

He walked alone, a mere speck striding across the pan-
orama of Palace Square. In front, the washed-out walls of
the General Staff building were crumbling like marzipan
in mercury drizzle. The green-and-white confection of the
Winter Palace provided a backdrop to the scene.

Tom recalled Iryna's parting rendition of Pushkin's dramatic lines from 'The Bronze Horseman':

The river fell back in rage and tumult
flooded the islands
grew fiercer and fiercer
reared up and roared
like a cauldron, boiled, breathed steam
and, frenzied, fell at last upon the town . . .

How different it was today, he thought. Sour rain, like yellow dribble from a cretin's drooling mouth, was falling. There was no cataclysmic flood like in 1824. It was so-postmodern, so insipid, so T S Eliot:

This is the way the world ends
This is way the world ends
This is the way world ends
Not with a bang but a whimper.

He stopped on the flat expanse, a solitary figure in a land of granite. A rusty van pulled up, its driver getting out, scurrying to an open doorway at the base of a wall that stretched away into a silk screen of fog and mist. Cranky hinges pierced the air as the door slammed. Young soldiers walked aimlessly back and forth, new recruits in ill-fitting greatcoats and circular hats, lighting cigarettes, laughing and swapping stories. They were at a loss for something to do. They eyed girls and hassled tourists as their only self-indulgence.

Tom felt like he was in the middle of an opera. From the Imperial Tsars to the insatiable Stalin, this square had been at the centre of Russia's political theatre. It was the very stage upon which the Revolution had opened, the epicentre of long-mourned tragedies, the consequences of which were still carved into the gaunt features passed down from generation to generation.

He was like a chess piece in some Grand Master's last

game, sensing his own decline, but also bearing witness to the debris of the moral and physical decay around him. He was thinking that all things come to an end. Empires and individuals alike experience the highs and lows of Spengler's lifecycle. All bloom, all die, and gradually fade into dust. How would this end, he asked himself, in fire or flood?

❖ The Europe-Asia bridge over the Ural River in Orenburg is the scene for a symbolic welcoming by President Babel, opening Russia up to the peoples of the East. He simultaneously announces the expansion of Orenburg's Tsentralny Airport to increase its capacity to meet the waves of migration from the south;

❖ Humanitarian agencies warn of the need to provide even more food and clothing for the mass exodus of people through Manzhouli in China's Xinjiang province into Zabaykalsky Krai;

❖ Standardised railway gauges are retro-fitted to speed up migrant transportation, funded jointly by the World Bank and Beijing;

❖ Frustrated with the Duma's inaction, nationalist vigilante groups launch Operation Optor (Repulse), a range of civil defence actions in Chelyabinsk, Orenburg, and Yekaterinburg.

Tom eyed a couple walking along the Gorokhovaya. The man was wearing a black leather jacket; his partner, a long fur coat. He wondered about their lives. Where did they live and work, and did they have enough money to get by? He realised that superficial outward signs were no indicator of real material wealth. Perfumes could be black-market, fashions could be replicated. There was an entire subculture working away under the surface, behind the shop fronts, in the back alleys around the city. Nevsky may have once showcased only the finest imported clothes, silverware, and furniture but the underground economy had still thrived in the shadows, because here appearance was all. Like everywhere else, image, perception, and the opulent display of wealth, once flaunted tastelessly in long stretch limos driving around the city centre, was expected; indeed, insisted upon. Nobody was exempt. Crass consumerism was a disease regardless of the recession. The little Sashas and Ludas were disgorged at birth into this pantomime of posturing. They had grown up surrounded by the notion of self-worth being measured by your paycheque and the idea that anything could be bought and sold. Everything was up for sale and everyone had a price. *Blat*, low level corruption, was everywhere and always would be.

Strolling through beating rain, moving on beyond the square, the tall buildings began to corral him. Damp, brown, brick faces were pressing in, looming large, almost threatening after the wide-open atmosphere of Dvort-sovaya Ploschad. To his left, the busy Nevsky disgorged itself into the muddy Neva. Locals and tourists were making for cover. To his right, the gravel gardens of the Admiralty stretched in a diarrhoea quagmire along the roadside. Raindrops were drilling gullies in the pathways, the wind whistling along the stone-ridged embankment. Tom wrapped his overcoat more tightly around himself and crossed the road in the face of oncoming traffic, seeking the shelter of the trees.

Teenage couples perched like love-birds on wooden benches, held hands, and talked furtively under the canopy of leaves. Their Goth-style makeup turned nervously towards him as he came along the path. Their pale, parasitical expressions eyed him suspiciously through dreary half-light. He noticed their conversations ceased as he approached, resuming as he passed, as if he represented the adult world they had come here to escape. Perhaps they thought he was a plainclothes policeman? He could see and smell the blue cigarette smoke drifting in the moist air. Behind him, the sound of a radio blared from wet undergrowth. He glanced over his shoulder. Above, the Admiralty's golden needle struck like a knife through the heart of a heavy black cloud, its baroque radiance dissipating in the hail. Uniformed militia guards took shelter under arched stone. A mother and her elfin daughter, wrestling with an umbrella, followed in his wake.

Two young girls were urging each other on, summoning up the courage to approach him. One held out a small, golden tin with red Cyrillic lettering on the lid.

'Would you like to buy best Russian caviar?' Tom looked at the object being thrust towards him. 'It is the very best in Russia', they continued, 'would you like to try?' They popped the top to reveal two small lumps wrapped in cellophane.

'What is it, Turkish delight?' he quipped.

'Call it what you like', one girl giggled. 'It is three hundred roubles . . . '

'I don't think so.' He went to walk on, but they stepped in front of him.

'This is a good deal.'

'I am sure it is, but I'm not interested, thank you.' Out of the corner of his eye, the Englishman caught sight of an older man, thick-set in tight leather jacket, his angry, boiled head emerging from the bushes. He shouted something to the girls and they tried to grab the Professor's sleeve. Tom pulled away, a runic cufflink tinkling to the ground. He moved quickly towards the main road at the rear of the Cathedral. The light was better there and commuters stood *en masse* waiting for trams. Behind him he could hear the pimp cursing, but no one paid him any mind.

- ❖ The heroin and cocaine trade is estimated to be worth 2.7 trillion roubles a year;
- ❖ Synthetic marijuana, known as 'spice', kills 2,000 people a month;
- ❖ Disciples of Vladimir Zhirinovsky assemble a coalition from across the United Russia, A Just Russia, and Yabloko political parties, standing shoulder to

shoulder under the great glass cupola, looking towards the Alexander Gardens in Moscow. Their
speeches highlight the impending final battle between Christianity and Islam, symbolically represented by the looming statue of St George and the
Dragon, close by;

❖ The city of Gudermes holds its second Islamic Caliphate Council which decrees that the *gazavat*, holy
war, demands the execution of all Christian soldiers held in the prisoner of war camps around Sa-
mashki;

❖ Heavy shelling is reported in Duba-Yurt, where a
small number of Russian troops, being supplied by
air, continues to hold out against overwhelming
odds;

❖ Satellite images identify thousands of Mohammed-
an fighters assembling in Ulus-Ket in the southern
lowlands of Chechnya.

The phone was ringing off the hook. Grigori's number
was flashing red on the digital panel. He threw off his
coat, deciding to call back later and risk irritating his host.
The place had been cleaned while he was out. He could
only guess what the chambermaid had made of all the
condoms stuck to the sheets.

When he did reluctantly listen to the messaging service, Grigori's monotone filled him with dread. It seemed
his Russian colleague was on his way over. He would not
take no for an answer. It was vital they spoke about security. Tom rolled over on the bedcover. There was something
ominous in every syllable Grigori uttered. By the time the
Professor had loosened his shirt collar and rinsed his face,
the doorbell was already sounding.

Hands still wet, the Englishman played with the lock-
chain. Grigori was staring back at him through the crack
in the door. 'It is well that you protect yourself', the Russian said reassuringly. 'There are people who will want to
disrupt the conference, intimidate speakers, you know the

kind of thing!'

'Certainly!' Tom reckoned that Grigori was no stranger to strong-arm tactics himself.

'I thought we could take a drink downstairs?'

Throwing on his jacket, Tom followed Grigori to the lift. They made ground level, stepping out into a lobby full of theatregoers sheltering from sheeting rain. Taking alcove seats in the Borsalino bar, Grigori continued being affable and polite, but Tom sensed a tightness in his movements, as if he was doing his best to hide his anxiety.

'Traditionalists like us are often misunderstood', he was saying. 'Our enemies try to present us as partisans for lost causes, soliloquies for dark movements.'

'Yes, I have experienced that', Tom agreed, 'and damned annoying it is too!' The Russian liked Tom's English expressions.

'Ivan Ilyin, the White's philosopher manqué, saw this from the outset. His *Knightly Way* meant religiously rooted state voluntarism. You see, he knew victory could only be achieved through spiritual resistance. For him, the war began in our own hearts.'

'"This test posed to every Russian soul the same direct question: who are you? By what do you live? What do you serve? What do you love?"'

'I see you are familiar with Ilyin's speech in Berlin.'

Tom affirmed with a cursory nod. 'Russia's situation, like that of many nation-states, may be as precarious right now as it was in 1923 when Ilyin spoke, but then, as now, there are signs of a stirring of nationalist forces. It often seems darkest before the dawn.'

'True!' Grigori was saying as the *maitre d'* swept past in a small claret waistcoat. 'Remember, I told you, we saw this start many years ago. By 1979, I already knew that Islamic fundamentalism spreading out from the Gulf was a major problem. I have friends who served in the Alpha and Zenith Special Forces in Kabul and arrested President Amin Halizullah in the Tajberg Palace.'

'Didn't they execute him on the spot?'

'Only after he was tried by a military tribunal. We were under no illusions. Even then we knew the CIA was funding the Mujahedeen with three billion dollars. And we know who finances the Arab Spring, ISIS, and the insurgents now.'

'The same people.'

'Who else? You can use the modern titles like neocons, cosmopolitans, and one-worlders if you want. Or you can call them usurers, Communists, or Bolsheviks. The labels and ideologies do not matter. If you scratch the surface, you find the answer. They use any means, financial or military, often interchangeably, if there is a profit to be had. Now, it suits their purpose to pull the strings of the Muslims. You know, we used to laugh about them. But look at your history books. In just over one hundred years after the death of their Prophet, the Muslims had taken over the Middle East, North Africa, and Spain. An empire larger than that of Augustus Caesar, and gained in half the time.'

'Well, Osama bin Laden did claim "the dissolution of the Soviet Union goes to God and the Mujahedeen in Afghanistan".' Grigori's eyes lifted to the ceiling in exasperation.

'And you see parallels with today?'

'It was the opening shots of the Clash of Civilisations!'

❖ Descendants of Russian religious schismatics are rounded up in the Bukhtarma Valley and deported by rail to the new border checkpoint at Orenburg;

❖ Archaeological sites like the Denisova Cave complex are destroyed by Islamic demolition squads seeking to extinguish evidence of the Seima-Turbino migrations, as they offend the Prophet;

❖ Dog-like domestic canid fossils are broken up by sledge-hammers in the Razboinichya Cave, for being 'unclean' in the eyes of God;

❖ Snow Leopards, Steppe eagles, and the black stork are hunted to near extinction as rumour that extracts from their spinal columns enhance male sexual performance spreads amongst Chinese homeopaths;

❖ Wild herds of Wisent and Ibex are factory farmed to meet the dietary needs of those migrating west;

❖ A large part of the inaccessible Ukok Plateau is turned into a restricted military centre, served only by the M52 highway;

❖ Evidence of the original Pazyry culture, such as the Bronze Age tomb of the fifth-century Scythian Ice Maiden, with elaborate tattoos and silk clothing, are dynamited to ensure no prior claim to ownership of the land is possible.

The bar was half empty, but Grigori was still watchful, eyes sweeping the room, ensuring no one overheard them. Over on the far side of the restaurant, a Negress with mother-of-pearl drop earrings sat at a piano, nicotine-stained fingers tickling blues standards from ivory. A waitress approached.

'Cappuccino', Tom asked nonchalantly. Grigori ordered a brandy. The Englishman was willing him to speak, to spit out what he had really come to talk about, noticing how his fingers had played with the paper napkin, twisting it into knots, as they had talked about the old war. Grigori continued with small talk as the waitress returned with their order.

'Please', Grigori insisted, gesturing for the receipt.

'Not on room?' the girl asked. Grigori looked directly into Tom's eyes.

'This is from me!'

At the other end of the bar, American tourists were tucking into pizza and babbling on about Brooklyn. Just for a moment, Tom wished the natives did not have to witness the eccentricities of such gauche Cold War warriors. They had won the peace by default, but were now in sharp decline. Obama's immigration mandates had all but bankrupted the 'Land of the Brave' and turned California into Disneyland for Latinos. Grigori began to speak as Tom ripped open a sachet of brown sugar.

'You know', he said, 'a very handsome poet called Sergei Yesenin slashed his wrists and hung himself in this hotel back in 1925. It is said that his final poem was written with his own blood.'

'How very melodramatic.'

'That is Russia for you', Grigori speculated. 'Always willing to make the grand gesture.' Tom saw his opportunity.

'And tell me what grand gesture would you like me to make?'

'So quick to the point!'

'No need to make a song and dance like your poet friend.'

'This is not British way?' Grigori was genuinely taken aback, laughing into his balloon glass.

'It's my way, let's forget stereotypes, *horosho*?' The Russian agreed, his eyes narrowing.

'It seems someone in my team has betrayed your whereabouts to the Bloc.'

Tom's eyes scanned the face of the man before him. 'Am I safe?'

'Probably not.'

'How dangerous are these people?'

'Well, they do not share our taste for academic freedom if it contradicts the wishes of their globalist masters.'

'Can you protect me?'

'Not 24/7.'

'But some of the time, right?'

'We have one man from Europe working with local supporters.'

'Europe?'

'I think he is Belgian by birth. He was trained by our brothers in Norway.'

'A political soldier?'

'A vanguardist!'

'I fully understand. I will take precautions. I am not

speaking until the final day, anyway, so it gives me plenty of time to sit in my room and prepare.'

'Yes, you are the plenary keynote.'

'Indeed!'

'But you will attend tomorrow, no?'

'Most certainly, there are several very interesting papers being presented. I am looking forward to it.'

'Good, I was very worried you would be scared off!'

'Well, of course I am concerned, but there is very little I can do about it now.'

Grigori's familiar guttural laugh broke out across the room causing heads to turn. 'That is more like it, famous British stiff upper lip!'

❖ In a replay of the Mongol invasion of 1238, the 900-year-old Collegiate Church of St Demetrios and the Cathedral of the Virgin are destroyed by Muslim terrorists;

❖ The Church of St Boris and St Gelb on the Nerl River is the scene of a mass rape of schoolgirls taken by force from a suburb of nearby Orgtrud;

❖ Twelve Orthodox priests are discovered hanging by the neck from the green and gold domes of the St Euthymius Monastery;

❖ Thousands gather around miracle-working icons at the Valdai Monastery, believing the end times have come.

Yulia Gavrilova, a plump and officious conference attaché, was ushering the delegates across the Astoria's lobby, clucking like a mother hen, counting them as they stepped up onto the metal footplate of a minibus with university markings. 'I'm afraid we have to take precautions', she was warning. 'RASH protesters are blockading the venue.'

'And the *politsiya*?' asked Ulrich Hoffman, striking a match to light the tobacco in the pipe bowl hanging before his grizzled chin.

'They have Kamaz personnel carriers.'

'That's 13mm armoured plate', the smoker coughed. Tom knew Hoffman to be an expert on the German Conservative Revolutionary Movement. A widely respected veteran of the identitarian movement, his family had been among the hundreds of thousands dispossessed and murdered along the length of the Danube after 1945.

'And Kord 6P50 machine guns', remarked Francine Karre, a dark-haired Parisian, reputed to be a rising political influence in France's Resistance. Her frequent appearances on Canal Plus defending militants like Sabine D'Orlac, known as *La Petroleuse*, had caused consternation in the Conseil Representatif des Institutions juives de France. Tom was particularly interested in her paper on Henry Coston. He had already read several of her monographs on Jacques Ploncard d'Assac and Yves Guerin-Serac, a founder of the OAS.

The driver banged the door, ready for their short journey down Nevsky. The sky was trying hard to rain, spitting Baltic phlegm at the windscreen.

'The Symposium', Yulia was explaining, 'will proceed as per the pre-arranged programme. Please', she said, handing out some pamphlets and timetables, 'these are some updates written in English.' The mini-bus heater was going full blast, filling the narrow cabin with a dry, unctuous odour bearing the taint of adolescent sports bags. Francine waved a folder in front of her face until another man in a brown trilby and tweed jacket asked in splintered Russian for it to be turned off. The English Professor eyed the man in the hat carefully before introducing himself.

'I don't think we've met?' The young man extended his hand.

'Peter Janssen', he said in accented Dutch English. Tom noticed the bulge in his jacket.

'Identitair Verzet?'

'Something like that!' They smiled knowingly at one another before Tom turned, looking out through the condensation on the window. The bridge to the left led over

to the *strelka*. The shops to the right were full of Western
products that no one could afford. A large red crane twisted clockwise on the English embankment, winching a
pontoon out over the river. Tom was thinking how he had
nearly rejected the offer to come to Russia as the bus took
a tight right onto the esplanade. Back then, his mind had
been set on flying to Buenos Aires rather than St Petersburg. An old contact had asked him to attend a live television debate on the controversy over paying a special pen-
sion to the surviving members of the nationalist student
group that had hijacked an Aerolineas flight and diverted
it to the Malvinas Islands, displaying the Argentine flag,
'in an act of national recovery and dignity' back in 1966.
Indeed, the Professor had always greatly admired Dardo
Cabo's Tacuara, so the offer was tempting. He recalled
reviewing his options in a Bayswater bedsit where he had
stayed the weekend with a young Ukrainian blonde called
Nadezhda. She had come to his attention at a meeting of
Carpatho-Pagans at Kings College. Later, they had a drink
together in Ye Olde Cheshire Cheese on Fleet Street, and
she confessed she was heavily involved in translation work
for the *Strike!* Website. He remembered she had been
wearing a black motorcycle jacket and carrying a copy of
Political Thought of the Ukrainian Underground. From that
moment, the East had become his magnetic north. Within
weeks, he was in contact with various Pan-Slavic groups,
and had been invited to give a paper in former Leningrad.

'The space technology industry was a big employer
here', Hoffman was explaining as he looked out over the
columns of people trudging like shell-shocked soldiers to
the front. 'A friend of mine at MIT wrote a book arguing
that if the CIS countries could harmonise their intellectual
creativity, their average GNP growth would be triple that
of the USA inside a decade.'

'I think things have deteriorated considerably', Peter
Janssen corrected. 'Russia's research in science and technology was recently evaluated as being equivalent to Holland's' Hoffman shook his head.

'Sign of the times.'

The bus came to a sudden halt outside a crenelated lemon wall, more like a castle under siege than a seat of learning. Outside, hordes of protesters hurled abuse, waved red flags, and tried to squeeze by the security cordon to throw rotten eggs at the van's windows. 'No more reactionaries like Prokhanov, Dugin, Glazyev, Fursov, Platonov, Narochnitskaya, and Father Tikhon—to hell with Den Fascisti . . . Shut down Pavlov—Rossiya is dead!' Tom glimpsed placards bearing the crossed-out faces of Viktor Alksnis, Yuri Vlasov, and Igor Artemov with the salutation 'RIP' scrawled beside their images. Yulia stood, her back arched, at the front of the bus.

'Please do not be concerned, we are perfectly safe', she said, to comfort herself as much as the guests. 'We will wait just one moment until the police have cleared a path.' Just then a rear window shattered, and a steel rod bounced about on the floor of the cabin. Janssen was up on his feet, hitting out at the hands pulling at the side of the vehicle, his blade slicing through fingers yanking on the metal.

'Go!' he was shouting. The driver pulled forward, the gates opening and the police sweeping down from the side-streets, beating at the crowd with riot shields and truncheons. Once they were inside, Yulia opened the sliding door. One by one they fell out, crumpled, shocked, and gasping for air. Janssen waited until everyone was clear, then slipped his knife back inside his sleeve. Tom followed the others through a side door into a narrow corridor where an old babushka took their bags and coats.

'Jesus Christ!' a Canadian from the Parti Unite Nationale shouted. 'How close was that?'

'This way, please', Yulia was saying, leading them up a stairway, circling the conference room's arched porticos. 'The building is protected!' Tom estimated there were over a hundred delegates crowded into the anteroom where hot drinks and digestive biscuits were being served. Taking a cup and spooning sugar, he looked over his shoulder.

Janssen was nowhere to be seen. The Professor figured he was supervising security.

'Anyone here from the USA?' someone called. 'I'm from Dallas.' Tom found himself talking to a short, fat American clutching a book entitled *Suprahumanism*. They exchanged business cards. Everyone was sizing each other up in the usual academic dick-measuring contest that these events inevitably became. The atmosphere was male and predatory. Young, female interpreters were getting plenty of unsolicited attention.

'I think some are hookers', the Texan said under his breath. 'See the butt on that one!' Tom looked with a degree of contempt at the paunchy wisecracker in front of him.

'That, my friend, is a product of the Shintashta gene pool!' Tom replied, casting a warm gaze over the slinky figure of a young student, 'the very same people who first mastered the horse, used the wheel, and gave birth to the Proto-Indo-European languages.'

'What is it with these women, man?' came the superficial reply. The American's eyes were bulging, lips moistening with the thought of unfastening her bra strap.

'You are looking at a time capsule. That is what women should look like. Your attraction is more than just physical. It is embedded in your DNA. Do you have any idea of her lineage?' The American was lost now, he was hoping to talk about copulation and alcohol. This lecture was unnerving him. 'She is a descendent of Vlasta, the famed female warrior who gave rise to the legend of the Amazons. Anna Michailivna and Queen Olga of Kiev who annihilated the Devlians.' He stopped for a moment to gauge the American's response. Sensing confusion, he decided to make it easier for him. 'And through her Rus heritage, she is Varangian. Their women stood side-by-side with the men in the shield wall. A lady called Marulla drew a line in the sand at Lemnos with the tip of her sword, before driving off Mohammed's Turks.'

'Awesome!'

'Quite!'

He sat on the window's ledge, flicking through vintage editions of *Nash Put* (Our Path), observing the networking. Peter Janssen was talking confidentially to a tall man with a wire running to his ear. Karre was flirting mercilessly with a swarthy Spanish liaison officer from the Populist Party. Behind him, in the courtyard, two lichen-covered statues stared blindly back in a tone of intellectual defiance. Memorials to academic heavyweights, he thought to himself. Names on Russian journals and research papers he would never read or comprehend. They were yesterday's men. Fighters like Janssen were today's men, a new breed. He smiled inwardly, thinking about where he fit in. What was it Eliot had written?

> We are the hollow men
> We are the stuffed men
> Leaning together
> Headpiece filled with straw. Alas!
> Our dried voices, when
> We whisper together
> Are quite meaningless
> As wind in dry grass
> Or as rat's feet over broken glass
> In our dry cellar
>
> Shape without form, shade without colour,
> Paralysed force, gesture without motion . . .

His reverie was broken by Yulia's harping. Her words fell irritatingly like cockroaches dropping from a straw roof. Hoffman was standing next to him, nicotine fingers stroking his chin.

'You look tired. Did you have an active night?'
'Yeah, you could say that.'
'You like Russian hospitality?'
'Yes, very much . . .'

'So I see . . .' Hoffman's eyes followed Tom's face as it slipped all over a pert young lady swinging by, coffee cup in hand. 'Now let me introduce you to Valentine, Rector of this august establishment. You know this is part of a new Arctogaia, a different sort of university. There was another in Kazakhstan, named by President Nursultan Nazarbayev after Lev Gumilev, the National Eurasian University. Valentine is a very important person, a leading light in the Vtorzhenie Movement, against Left and Right, a recognised authority on the anthropological aspects of the Don Basin.' They walked together to the lecture theatre. Hoffman unbuckled the pipe stem from his mouth, licking cracked lips as Yulia came towards them, brandishing her umbrella like a medieval weapon.

'Come, come, honoured guests, it is time, please!'

Entering the auditorium, they were hit by a wall of light. The atmosphere crackled. The hair on Tom's arms stood on end. You could practically taste the tungsten at the back of your throat.

'Where do we sit?' Yulia overheard Hoffman's question and orchestrated them with the metal tip of her umbrella to some seats midway across the third aisle.

'Reserved for you!' They clambered along, causing a Mexican wave of shuffling knees and jostling briefcases, assuming their places next to Iryna, Tom's guide around the Peter and Paul fortress. 'I see you are a keen student', she gushed. 'Welcome!'

'Indeed, *spasibo.*' By the time the audience had settled, the hall was impressively full. Besides representatives from the Zaporozhian Sich, sitting under a bright red Cossack flag with a Maltese Cross above the stage, there were leading figures from Golden Dawn, Germany's NPD, Austria's Freedom Party, Hungary's Jobbik, the Lithuanian Unity Party, the National Alliance Latvia, the Progress Party Norway, the Danskernes Parti from Denmark, the Sweden Democrats, Bulgaria's Natsionalen Sayuz Ataka, National Union Attack, the Finnish Perussuomalaiset, the True Finns, the National Front from France, and an assortment of British nationalist groups. Valentine Bondarenko, the Rector, stepped up to the microphone and began to speak. His willow-thin features and speckled scalp were sweating in the spotlights. In his opening remarks, he ventured to say that in the past, such a multi-national gathering of White advocates would never have occurred. 'But that time of suspicion and division has come to an end. We stand straight and tall', he said proudly, 'and speak out loudly for our ancestry!' The audience responded with a standing ovation. Waiting for the exuberance to subside, he concluded, 'Now it is my pleasure to invite our respected colleague, Vasili Burov, to commence proceedings with his introductory lecture on "Contemporary Misconceptions of the politics of Belarus".' A further wave of applause drum-tapped the speaker to the podium. A plasma screen lit up, and Burov's right hand squeezed the computer controls like a well-drilled Tupolev fighter pilot. Two hours and three presentations later, the first break was announced. Taking the opportunity, Tom slipped away while the other delegates milled around talking, dipping malted biscuits in sweet black chai.

3.

... to discover where this exquisite creature lived
who seemed to have flown straight down from
heaven onto the Nevsky Prospekt, and who would
probably fly away ...—Gogol

Hard rain pelted the college cloister. The muddy rivulets
were running zig-zag cracks on the path. Tom was sheltering under a wild cherry when he first noticed the whisper
trails of her brown hair, then the determined step of
leather boots, textbooks clutched firmly to her breast.
Coming out from under peeling bark, scabrous flesh blowing like a leper's limbs, he fell in stride behind, eyes focussed on the suede shoulderbag swinging at a sleekly-
curved hip. Following through arched gateways, along
cobbled courtyards, he was mesmerised by the rhythmic
click-clack of heels ricocheting like sniper bullets off
stone.

   Soon they were past security, out through the gates into the city, making their way across a footbridge adorned
with four gold-winged griffins. The Nevsky Prospekt, long,
straight and uncompromising, beckoned. She was walking
with purpose, stepping off the bridge, favouring the canal
bank. The protests were dissipating, and only small groups
hovered in distant doorways, shut off behind a police cordon, yelling profanities through the smoke and rain. He
was about thirty metres behind, long moleskin coat flapping open as a carpet of crisp red leaves swept the bridge's
woodwork.

   The canal was cut with military precision. Black water
slapped mouldy slabs, brickwork crowned with ornate
railings. Above, shuttered windows were locked tight

against acrid air. A thick Baltic mist rolled towards the Neva, where the golden spire of the Admiralty spiked the skyline like a heroin syringe.

Swelling crowds greeted them at Gostiny Dvor, clusters of commuters waiting for streetcars that ran on webbed wires. Oily tracks curled over bridges, crossing Nevsky's canals at irregular intervals. He found himself pushing through herds of women, men smoking foul black cigarettes, lining up for trams. The grizzle of gasoline filled his lungs. Chemical rat-bites had nibbled at the nearby Mikeshin monument of Catherine the Great. People came from far and wide, spilling out of cafés, bars, and boutiques onto the wet boulevard. It was a forest of dripping umbrellas and flickering neon.

He wondered what the Russian word for stalker was? Whether she had even noticed him? A band of Roma with swarthy arms, tattoos, and outsize hoods swaggered by, giving him the eye. He buttoned his coat and turned up the collar. Raindrops were running down his neck. The street kids moved on, distracted by easier pickings coming out of a gift shop, speaking like Elvis Presley.

She was gliding gracefully past the scaffolding surrounding the town hall tower, still smoke-stained following a recent incendiary attack. A dog barked furiously. Sharp, yellow teeth snapped at his knees, until a flat face wrapped in a ragged shawl yanked its chain. He sidestepped the beast, his gaze fixed on the girl, who was now looking for a point to cross the Griboedova. A Russian Little Red Riding Hood lost in the wintry colonnades of the Kazan Cathedral.

Tracking her to a sports café, he pushed on the swing door, hung his coat, then walked across the polished wood floor. 'May I join you?'

Big, grey-blue eyes travelled over him, evaluating this stranger for threat and opportunity. He estimated she was in her mid-20s. Her elegant white throat was wrapped in a roll-neck jersey, lilac fingernails tightly curled under a porcelain chin. He thought for a second that her glance was tinged by a sense of distance, that remote demeanour which attractive young women often affect for the purpose of self-preservation. But instead, she slid aside textbooks by Gumilev and Panarin, gesturing for him to sit. Doctor Hunter took the green light and took the empty chair.

A finger travelled to her lips, tossing back her hair as she spoke. 'You are from London, yes?'

'You speak very good English.'

'Also German, French, and some Italian.'

'I'm afraid I speak very little Russian!'

'That is because English is the world language.'

'Well, that's my excuse, truth is I'm lazy!'

She let out a bubble of laughter. 'I thought that was the Americans?'

'We blame them for everything else. Sure, why not?'

'I'm Ekaterina.' She held out a demur hand, which he accepted, thinking how soft it was in his. No wedding ring.

'I'm Tom', he replied. 'Glad to meet you.'

'And are you enjoying your stay in Piter?'

'Yes, I am on a lecture tour, speaking at the conference.' His head moved sideways, indicating the way back towards the Cathedral. Tom reached out, lifting her books. 'May I?'

'Gumilev taught in the history faculty at Leningrad before being denounced and sent to Norilisk. This book, *Ethnogenesis of the Biosphere of the Earth*, is seminal.'

'And the son of the Silver Age poets Nikolai Gumilev and Anna Akhmatova!'

The girl's lip curled with surprise. He winked.

'And Panarin's work *Strategic Instability in the 21st Century* is a critical analysis of globalisation.'

'I prefer his demolition of Fukuyama's thesis in *The Revenge of History*.'

'Or perhaps *Orthodox Civilisation in a Globalised World*?'

'Indeed, I think that won awards?'

'The Solzhenitsyn Prize of 2002!'

'Ah, the great Alexander Isayevich. I am very fond of his novels.'

'"Should someone ask me whether I would indicate the West such as it is today as a model to my country, frankly I would have to answer negatively. No, I could not recommend your society in its present state as an ideal for the transformation of ours"', she quoted from Solzhenitsyn's 1978 Harvard speech. Tom smirked and made the mistake of engaging in a contest. Scratching his head, he replied: '"A decline in courage may be the most striking feature that an outside observer notices in the West today. The Western world has lost its civic courage . . . such a decline in courage is particularly noticeable among the ruling and intellectual elites . . . from ancient times decline in courage has been considered the beginning of the end."'

Ekaterina was already one step ahead. '"Without any censorship, in the West fashionable trends of thought and ideas are carefully separated from those which are not fashionable; nothing is forbidden, but what is not fashionable will hardly find its way into periodicals or books or be heard in colleges. Legally your researchers are free, but they are conditioned by the fashion of the day. There is no open violence such as in the East; however, a selection dictated by fashion and the need to match mass standards frequently prevents independent-minded people from giving their contribution to public life. There is a dangerous tendency to form a herd, shutting off successful development."'

'Bravo, I see you are a real scholar!'

'My grandfather has a big library. Lots of books by Nikolay Danilevsky and his thoughts on civilisation, even more on Lev Alexandrovich Tikhomirov and the Slavic Commune.'

'His selection is eclectic.'

'It tends to challenge the cultural hegemony of the current dominant sect!'

'A true disciple.'

'I am a discerning student. I see the smoke and mirrors.'

'You mean people like Max Horkheimer, Leo Lowenthal, and Franz Neumann?'

'I see you critique the Frankfurt School of thought.'

'Nothing but politically correct social saboteurs!'

'Shush', a sharp finger went to her lips. 'Lenin would have had you shot!'

'Isn't he lying in a vat of embalming fluid in the Kremlin?'

'Please, your respect, my mother was a young Pioneer', she said in mock anger. 'I'll have you sent on the Vladimirka to Siberia.'

He leaned forward to whisper, 'Would you take the trip with me?' Another bubble of nervous laughter. Then Tom added more realistically, 'Would you like to attend the conference?'

'No, I'm visiting my grandfather. He's not been well.'

'I'm sorry to hear that. I'm speaking there and was trying to impress you.' Ekaterina reached into the bag slung over the back of her chair and took out a flyer printed in Russian.

'Everyone knows about what's going on at the university.' He looked at the material she handed him and pointed out his name on the list of dignitaries. It was her turn to smile. 'I hope the Reds don't get you!'

Tom sat with his back to the wall, following her eyes around the café, studying her every move. The place was buzzing. He overheard some English being spoken through the crescendo of chatter and jazz-fusion. A woman strolled by, babe in arms. Businessmen from a local office were gathered, huddled in blue clouds over an ashtray. Catching the attention of a sullen waitress, Tom and Ekaterina ordered borsch and sparkling water. Someone dropped a set of plates across the far side of the room. White chips of crockery splintered on the hard floor.

'How long are you staying?' she asked, as the waitress

came back with their order. He waited for the tray to be set down and loosened the caps on green Evian bottles. Pouring for Ekaterina, they watched as the slices of lemon rose in the glug of water.

'My return flight is scheduled for the 23rd.'

'When does your visa end?'

'One month.'

'Multiple entry?'

'No', he said. 'Your precious authorities have imposed new controls.'

'Which hotel?'

'Astoria.'

'That is a good hotel.'

'Close to the Hermitage and the embankment.'

'Have you been out on the river?'

'No.'

'You should, it's beautiful!'

'Will you show me?'

There was a second's hesitation. 'Yes, I'd enjoy that very much.' Unfolding cream napkins, they lifted curved spoons, making uneasy eye contact as they took steaming borsch.

Tom accompanied Ekaterina on a bone-shaking metro ride out to Ulitsa Dzybenko. Mounting cracked steps, they were greeted by jutting balconies, hanging slack like broken concrete jaws, looking down from Stalinist apartment blocks. Sliding between traffic, they entered a south-facing tenement, just as sunset threw a bloodshot eye over the Kurpatov tractor factory. She was moving quickly up the hallway, dying sunrays sending lasers through the prism of shattered glass. He watched the amber light play through her hair, glowing fingers caressing the nape of her neck.

'Marina was a language student at Herzen University, like me', she was saying. 'A dear friend and good to meet. Many from my class will be here tonight. We talk, listen to music, exchange books and downloads by our favourite bands. X Terror, Wavex, and Trezvy Reikh.'

'I'm glad to see the real Russia at last', he confessed. 'I was beginning to feel like a tourist.'

Ekaterina stopped in front of a blue metal shutter. Then, after a quick call on her mobile, the door clanked open, the corridor filling with Iron Order's rhythmic drumming. As they entered, Tom estimated that the flat was hosting ten or twelve people. They were mainly journalists, teachers, and would-be artists. Marina emerged from the lounge, kissing his companion on each cheek, shaking Tom's hand with a certain degree of formality, before ushering them into a small kitchen, where she uncorked a fresh bottle.

'Chilean', she smiled, 'Very lovely taste. I prefer French, I think?' They were soon joined by her partner, Nikita, a serious young man with a brooding intellect. He wore black shoes, black jeans, and a black turtleneck jersey. His crow-like eyes and pale skin were offset by the obligatory goatee worn by all the city's intelligentsia. Thin fingers played with the metal frames of round spectacles.

'Hi', he said. 'Your first time?' Tom nodded, sipping his drink. 'I went to London once when I was young. I stayed in Bermondsey by the river. My father did some work for a bank there. He told me I should come with him, chance of a lifetime.'

'And was it?' Nikki looked surprised by the question.

'Yes, of course. London is a most fine cultural city. Much to do. Very much to see!'

'Which was your favourite?' By now a crowd had gathered, listening to their hero talking to the surprise guest. 'Katja!' people were calling, throwing their arms around her, looking with curiosity at the stranger. They smiled, giving each other knowing looks, whispering their opinions.

'Is he looking for a Russian bride?' someone asked. 'He looks that way.'

'No, he's a spy!'

'We'd better send for Lev Ovalov, he knows all about MI6.'

Nikki pulled a cork on another bottle and re-filled their glasses. Marina dragged Ekaterina into a corner where she was immediately surrounded by gushing girls, lighting cigarettes and flicking long hair.

'They are joking', he said. 'Lev Orvalov is a hero from old Russian espionage stories. I am nothing like him. Anyway I prefer books by Ivan Shevtsov!' Tom waved his apology aside. 'You were asking about my favourite exhibit?' For a moment the Russian looked perplexed. 'Most certainly the National Portrait Gallery.' The Professor signalled his approval. 'I recall sailing down the river between Westminster and Greenwich. We drank black beer in a pub by the Cutty Sark.'

'The Gypsy Moth.'

'Named for another boat! Are all English people on the sea?'

'We're an island nation!'

'Indeed. But it is being taken over by Brussels.'

'You have fears for my country?'

'England is also changing', the young man asserted, throwing back a mouthful of wine, 'and not for the best.' Tom agreed. 'We saw those riots and who was to blame. I saw the way your BBC tried to hide who was responsible for the sex trade of children in Rotherham, Manchester, and Sheffield. Our Russian media are less politically correct. We understand all.'

'You do?'

'We do, but we have our own problems from the East.'

'Do you think Russia will implode?'

Nikki grimaced. 'Russia is stuck in the old debate between the Westernisers and the Eurasianists. Look, we have hundreds of ethnic subgroups and regional languages in our territory, but whatever argument you make, people like the Kyrghyz and Ingush are still *inorodtsy*, aliens. For Vitaly Aveyanov, a former Director of the Institute of Dynamic Commemoration, the Russian Empire should expand, but to do so it must "recruit new and good people". The point is the current ruling elite is always go-

ing to be split on ethnic lines, with members at different
times seizing the assets of the Union of Republics for personal gain, ignoring the interests of the nation as a whole.
For Aveyanov, "the myth of empire is needed as a so-
called attracter to win support for achieving that goal".'

'Careful, you are beginning to sound like our old friend
Zhirinovsky. Didn't he say, "We should think about saving
the White race because today the white race is the minority in the world. It is a minority that needs to be protected
and saved. If we don't fight against this danger—the Islamic danger, the Asian danger—then in the future we
will have a religious danger and, finally, religious wars
where we will be swamped by what is called the yellow
peril"?'

'Sometimes wise words come from the mouths of fools.
He also predicted all those years ago that "Russia can play
a historic role in saving the world from the spread of Islam, from the spread of international terrorism . . . Trust
me there is a long tradition of Muslim caliphs taking
Christian wives, or themselves being born of a white
mother. You see they were our mothers, daughters and
sisters, captives from Mongol, Arab or Persian raids. That
is why we must fight these hordes of Tamerlane once
more, resist them unto our last breath".'

'His assassination was a sad day.'

'An inevitable day. Such voices must be silenced.'

'But your voices are not being silenced, we hear your
protests as far away as London.' Nikki grew in confidence.

'Yes, on the fourth of November, the Feast Day of our
Lady of Kazan and the anniversary of Michael Romanovs'
expulsion of the Poles from Moscow, we gather under the
black, white, and yellow pennants, not only here but also
in Saratov, Perm, Ulyanovsk, Cheboksary, and Mur-
mansk.'

'Have you been to the monuments to Minin and
Pozharsky in Nizhny Novgorod and Moscow?'

'Marina organises the dance festival in Nizhny. We all
watched Alexander Dugin on programmes like *Vremya*

and *Chto de-lat.*'

'Does he make good viewing?'

'Well, when they let him speak. He used to appear on *Moment Istiny* and *Russkiy vzglyad*, too! The Eurasianists are right about some things, like the United States and the EU wanting to establish new states ranging from Kosovo-style NATO protectorates to Islamic emirates from the Black to the Caspian Sea. That is why they sustained a military presence in Afghanistan and threatened Iran, to keep control over energy resources, while denying Russia access to the Mediterranean. The response was that we seized Crimea. By overrunning Western Ukraine, they further weaken and fragment the Russian state, challenge our dominance over the Eurasian heartland, run arms, deal in narcotics, and encourage migrants.'

'Have you read Dugin's *Fourth Political Theory*?'

'Yes, but you know I'm unsure about some of Dugin's positions. At first we were all very excited about the Evraziia Youth Movement. They had forty or more offices in Russia and ten or so internationally. He seemed to be influential with Putin, but all this talk of Arctogaia and Hyperborea was lost on many. Sergey Glazyev, for example, says the Eurasianist ideology amounts to one simple idea—we are all tied to a common historical fate, and we need to build a common future while respecting each other's sovereignty and observing the principles of mutual benefit, emphasising our historical kinship. This is what differentiates us from EU expansion. The EU practises a methodology of double standards, applying force, fraud, and political technologies. Unlike both Glazyev and Dugin, I believe in a European ethnic identity and am against Russia's multicultural imperialism.' Tom saw how these fundamental differences troubled the young guy standing in front of him.

'I remember an interview Dugin did in *Elementi* in 1995 with the former Iranian Ambassador to the Vatican, Muhammad Masjd Jamei, about how the Orthodox and Muslim worlds share common problems and common enemies. "With the fall of the Communist regimes in Eastern Europe, Western militarists are attempting to destroy the last few remainders of national, cultural, and religious independence. From their point of view, Islam and Orthodoxy are the essence of a power bloc whose existence is incompatible with their plans. It is for this reason that such efforts are expended on the weakening or even the destruction of these two religions".'

'I do like Dugin's alter ego Hans Ziver's *Tribute to the the History of the Moscow Underground* and that verse from "Moscow 1982":

Here strict pattern eyelashes,
Stings mascara,
And black darkness hangs,
In the city of the Dead Souls.'

'Ha, have you ever read, *It's Me, Eddie*, by Eduard Limonov?'

'No, is it good?'

'Very different. He also wrote *Memoir of a Russian Punk*, *The Wild Girl*, and *The Other Russia.*'

'I'm familiar with his politics but don't know his fiction.'

'Then you are missing something, my friend, many of the people here tonight were on the Dissenter's March in 2007 when he was detained by the authorities. Others fought with the Fratria Movement at the Iberian Gate in 2010. Some are White Rex activists, others are National Bolsheviks. Danila, over there is a big admirer of Tesak. Sasha, his brother, is a member of the Patriots of Russia Party, the group who took over Pionerskaya Square in 2011.'

'And Limonov was arrested at the Dissenter's March, right?'

'Yes. But when he was an émigré in the States, he was heavily influenced by Lou Reed and Charles Bukowski. After a period in Paris, he returned to the Motherland and founded an incendiary political news-sheet called *Limonka,* you would say, *hand grenade.'*

'Original!'

'So original it was said he was disseminating illegal and immoral information!'

'And was there any truth in the charge?'

'Well, he was imprisoned in 2001 for terrorism and trading in illegal weapons!'

'And would you ever do that?'

'Do what? Organise an armed revolt in northern Kazakhstan?'

'Get involved with armed groups, wherever?'

'Look, Limonov's National Bolshevik Party was banned by the Supreme Court but it changed into the Other Russia. Dugin was right when he said, "If the European New Right chooses us, that means it chooses the barbarian element . . . our people do not only go to meetings or fight at the barricades, they also go to real wars, for instance Moldova, or to Yugoslavia." There are over sixty White Power bands in this country today. Their fan base has a lot of muscle. We are fans of Zyklon B and Bezumnye Usiliya. I saw Kolovrat's open air concert in Bolotnaya Square. All of us attend rallies on National Unity Day.'

'Arming the *narod khoziain.'*

'The Master People.' Nikkin was surprised. 'I see you know some Russian.'

'I believe in the *Rossiki Natsiia.'*

Nikki raised a toast. 'To the *Russkii Dom!'*

'The Russian home', Tom echoed with a clink of his glass.

❖ Suicide bombers kill 196 and injure 317 in sporadic attacks on the Moscow Metro;

❖ A government report which concludes that drug remittances fund over 2 million Azers living in Russia is suppressed in the public interest;

❖ The last Yazidis of northwestern Iraq, inheritors of ancient pre-Islamic traditions, are finally hunted down and exterminated;

❖ Jews and Muslims come together in the shadow of the Dome of the Rock in a show of public solidarity against world-wide racism;

❖ CIA and Mossad operatives are killed in action in eastern Ukraine;

❖ In Baku, where medieval mosques sit side-by-side with dilapidated Soviet apartment blocks and new glass office towers, gun-running, narcotics, and human trafficking becomes the motor of the economy through Tabriz, Samarkand, and down towards Kabul;

❖ Central Asian oil and gas producers provide free energy to Israel under terms negotiated by the World Bank.

They chatted over *bliny* filled with honey about a Russky Verdikt campaign to free Yevgenia Khasis from the Mordvinian camps. 'She is our Sabine D'Orlac!' Nikita became animated. 'An icon for people like Vladimir Kvachkov's People's Liberation Front.' Ekaterina pulled away from her crowd, introducing a young man with sky-grey eyes.

'Vladimir is a writer', she said. 'But now he works for Ernst and Young.'

'I do accounting ledgers', he added.

Tom feigned interest to indulge Ekaterina. 'What sort of stuff do you write?'

'Political.' He thrust a sheaf of papers into Tom's hands. 'This is an English copy. You can read if you want.'

'You wrote all this?'

'Katja says I write more in European taste. She helps me translate into French and British.' Tom looked admiringly at her.

'You must have great faith in his talent?'

She blushed. 'I have confidence', she said, grabbing Vladimir by the arm and giving him an affectionate squeeze.

'What's it called?' Tom asked before turning the cover.

'*Dog*', Vladimir replied. 'It's about times when I was a child.'

'She is your muse?' he hinted, trying to evaluate the depth of their relationship.

'*Da!*'

'Which authors influence you?'

'I try to be like Valentin Rasputin.'

'Never heard of him.'

'He was a writer from the Village Prose School, like Victor Astafiev and Fyodor Abramov.'

'No clearer.'

'He wrote *Live and Remember.*'

'Sorry?'

'He was from Siberia!'

Tom shook his head.

'He writes like Shishkin paints', Ekaterina interrupted.

'So who do you like to read?' Vladimir was nothing if not persistent.

'Kafka!' Tom was trying to lighten the atmosphere.

'You like Kafka?'

'Very much so. "Metamorphosis" is my favourite short story. But tell me, what English writers do you like?'

'Joy Division.'

'Ian Curtis, you mean?'

'Did you meet him?'

'No, I never had the pleasure. He committed suicide when I was still a kid.' He looked towards Ekaterina. 'I'm not really that old, you know.' There was a plaintive tone in his voice which the Russians took for a joke, but was more of a subconscious appeal for acceptance.

'What about Death in June?'

'Yes, I've seen them several times.'

'Have you heard Egor Letov's Grazhdanskaia Oborona or Sergei Zharikov's band DK?'

Tom was about to expound on the virtues of the neo-folk scene when Ekaterina put a hand to his mouth. A guitar was being strummed. The first chords of *Rodina* filled the room.

'Quiet, Olga is going to sing!'

Later Nikki dimmed the lights and Marina draped a thin silk scarf over a table lamp. The guests' faces were luminous in the flickering candlelight as they sat in armchairs, or stood, backs against the wall, sipping wine and vodka in front of a green flag bearing the image of Svantevit riding a white horse. In the middle of the room, a poltergeist of blue smoke hovered over a chocolate cake. They sang happy birthday to Viktoria, a dark-haired woman with a pinched white face and crimson lips.

As the last verse died away, she cut the cake, eyes moist with emotion, thin hands passing generous portions. Then the rock music was fired up again: Denis Maydanov's 'The Evil Approaches'. There was much hugging and kissing. People danced and fluted glasses were smashed in the fireplace. One young man sat on the floor, propped up by a pile of books. He was trying to sing, a tuneless monotone coming from his jerking head. A girl flung a cushion and then a shoe, telling him to be quiet. The drunk ignored her, taking a long pull on a flaring spliff.

Over in the far corner, Viktoria lay asleep by an electric fire. Her hair caught like sticky flypaper to her glistening face. Vladimir staggered across the room, an empty glass helicoptering in front of him. He kept mouthing, 'A drink . . . do you want to drink with me?'

'You're dry', Marina shouted, lifting a vodka bottle. Ekaterina reached to push it away.

'Vlad's had too much.'

'Hey, you're not his mother', Marina exclaimed. 'Let him enjoy himself!'

'*Da*', Vladimir said. 'More!' His muse shrugged in resignation. Vladimir threw back a glass and began to pour again. His eyes struggled to focus, squinting at the English Professor malevolently. 'So you think I can't write?' he began to say in broken English, making a fist. 'I bet you think I'm nothing good!'

'Why do you always do this?' Ekaterina pleaded.

'Do what?' he asked.

'Drink and upset yourself.' Vladimir's finger pointed straight at Tom.

'He thinks he's better than me!'

'I barely know you', the Englishman replied defensively.

'Oh, he knows you', Nikki said, swooping in to guide Vladimir away to the other side of the room. 'You're another man to come between him and Katja.' Marina clapped.

'It's true', she said. 'Vlad loves you!'

'But we're just friends', she stammered.

'He loves you', Marina confirmed emphatically, 'He confessed it to me at the festival.'

4.

I felt an abnormal, mean secret stirring of pleasure
in going back home to my corner from a debauched
St Petersburg night . . .—Fyodor Dostoevsky

Tom descended, his shoes beating an unhurried drumroll
on chipped concrete. The roar of car engines resounded in
the tenement. Mesmerised by the tadpole-like raindrops
sliding over splintered glass, his cold fingers played with
the slip of paper where Ekaterina had scratched her mobile number.

He pulled up his collar and stepped into the wind. In
the distance, a bridge curled over the canal, office lights
reflecting like koi carp in dark water, the night groaning
through loose guttering.

❖ In a direct reversal of historian Michael Khordarkov-
   sky's description of Russia's relentless advance east
   across the steppe in the 1600s, the former colonisers
   become the colonised as population forecasts project
   that by 2030 there will be 250 million new Muslim immigrants living in Russia;
❖ Single Chinese men are the largest demographic visiting Ukraine, ostensibly searching for wives;
❖ Traditional village feasts along the Darya River are disrupted by rampaging Muslim youth;
❖ Human trafficking and sex slavery, practised so openly
   on the Shomali Plain, spreads across eastern Russia.
   Unconfirmed numbers of women are reported as
   committing suicide while thousands of girls are
   shipped in open trucks to Jalalabad;
❖ Mosques in Perm Krai, the Qosarif Mosque in Kazan,

and the Central Mosque of Karachaevo-Cherkessia receive multi-million endowments from the Gulf;

❖ Over 320,000 Muslims travel from Russia to attend the
hajj in Mecca;

❖ Al Faath veterans, formerly active as the 055 group in
Bosnia, are reported to be carrying long ritual knives in
order to slit throats and skin people in Khabarovsk;

❖ *Russia Today* secretly films meetings in Kandahar
which implicate the Pakistani government in supplying
munitions to the Taliban;

❖ Moscow's Dormition Cathedral is bombed by Wahhabi
extremists. The Head of the Union of Russian Muslims,
speaking at the Imam Khatyb Madrassa, says: 'There is
only room for our faith in Russia.'

At the corner of Prospekt Bolshevikov and Ulitsa
Krylenko, a group of feral Khachi youngsters wearing
black scarves and bored expressions stood like sentinels.
The Professor tried to walk by, acting as nonchalantly as
possible, conscious they might scent his instinctive fear.
For a moment, he tried to imagine himself in their shoes;
a leather wallet, mobile phone, and a Western passport
had real, convertible street value. It was certainly better
than ABSOLYuT BANK in these uncertain times. There
were no administration charges, just an exchange of goods
in a dank stairwell followed by hours of drug-fuelled may-
hem in the clubs. Ignorant, agitated, and high, the sight of
a well-dressed foreigner walking alone on an isolated
street would naturally excite their predatory appetite.
They began calling to him, asking who he was.

A scooter ripped by at full throttle. Legs kicked out and
a bottle smashed on the road ahead. Should he respond,
or would they recognise bravado and charge? When he
heard his name called, he became anxious. This was no
chance encounter. They knew of him and no doubt why
he was in St Petersburg. His knuckles whitened. The 250's
engine resounded off brick walls. Tom crossed the road,
trying to retrace his steps. The buzz-saw sound of the

scooter circled. He could just make out the hump-back silhouette of someone riding pillion, sliding off the seat as the bike skidded in a squeal of grating rubber. Then, a clenched fist stupefied his would-be assailant, sending his attacker reeling. Before Tom knew what was happening, Janssen was standing beside him, a swift blade gleaming in starlight.

'Get behind me!' Janssen bellowed. Tom followed orders, hands protecting his pockets, edging to the curb. His protector swept the gap between them and the street gang with his scarab knife. For several seconds, Tom stood sweating, knowing it was only a matter of time before they rallied and moved forward *en masse*. Suddenly, a car pulled up and Janssen shouted for him to get in. With doors slamming and beer bottles raining down, they sped off along Shotmana towards the river.

Inside the car, Tom shook his head and breathed a sigh of relief, whilst their driver cursed about foreign kids running wild on the streets. It was better in the old days, he was saying. 'All the stealing and the violence started when the outsiders came.'

'Thank you', Tom said, turning towards Janssen. 'I never expected . . . '

'I was out for a walk', Janssen joked. 'Just happened to be coming along.' They drove down Dalnevostochnyy, crossing the Neva at Lomonosovskaya, heading for Elizarovskaya and the centre. As they turned off Ligovsky Prospect into Nevsky, Tom pointed right rather than left and said he wanted to be dropped at the Hotel Moskva. 'Are you sure?' Janssen asked.

'Yes, it'll be ok.' Tom had remembered Anna and Oksana telling him they worked the hotel foyer. Adrenalin was better than Viagra. The Professor felt the pulse of blood to his groin. The threat of violence had scared but also excited him. He was hungry for sex and wanted to spread a woman's legs to celebrate his close call. 'Thanks again', he said, hoping Janssen would not offer to accompany him. The driver looked for Janssen to give him the nod. They were circling the Alexander Nevsky monument in front of the Moskva, its red, translucent signage casting a warm arc over the motorway bridge. The road rose, spanning the narrowing Neva before heading east towards Moscow.

'See you, friend!' He waved as he threw open the door. Janssen tipped his cap knowingly, commanding the driver to move on. Tom strode into the lobby and made for the bar. Taking a seat, he ordered whisky with ice before taking a look around. Nearby, a group of young girls sat talking behind a palisade of Sobranie cigarettes. They were wearing bright leather jackets, tight mini-skirts, and high-heeled shoes. To their left sat two or three single girls, reading magazines and drinking herbal tea. One in particular caught his eye. She had the long limbs and javelin features of a model. Her hair was pulled back in an Arabian ponytail, a glossy copy of *Tatler* draped over her knee. After a few moments he turned his head to check for further shopping options. Three more women, high cheekedboned, educated types, sat on stools in an adjacent booth. There was a redhead girl, a bleach blonde, and a girl with what he took to be a Chinese pedigree, hovering, looking for business. By the time his drink arrived, the girl in the blue top had come across. Her face, side-lit by the table's candle flame, struck him as simply sublime. She had a fulsome mouth, shining eyes, and snowy skin.

'If you want I can come to room for massage and sex', she said, 'One hundred euro!'

'I don't have a room.'

Her smile subsided. 'I know place, but it is twenty euro more.'

'OK, please take a seat.' She sat and watched him drink. 'What's your name?'

'What would you like it to be?'

'Cecilia', he ventured, remembering the shuddering frigidity of his former wife. A look of casual acceptance came over her face. 'Private joke', Tom ventured by way of explaining his choice. He noticed her glass was empty and ordered a celery juice which she gulped quickly, pulling threads from between her teeth.

'I don't know how you can drink that stuff.' His eyes watching her wet tongue caress her lips.

'Good for skin and no calories', she replied. Then she stood up, running her hands down her hips. 'No thickness, you see?'

'But it tastes like grass!'

'But I look good, no?' Tom was studying the loose cut of her Wranglers, its hang revealing the soft roundness of the girl's flat belly and the top of a white cotton thong.

'Then you do suffer for your looks.'

'Better to have good face and nice figure in my business', she suggested, wiggling her pert backside.

'That is true. Tell me, are you an actress?' It was a ritual compliment but it was appreciated.

'Sometimes I have done TV', she said, lying. He leaned forward to smell her perfume.

'You smell expensive.'

'Kenzo Flower', she murmured sexily. 'It is by Guerlain.' Pulling at a red rubber band, she shook her hair out over slight shoulders. 'You like?' she asked provocatively.

'I like.' A pause. 'Everything!'

A few minutes later he found himself being led outside. Before him, the noble statue of Alexander, Prince of Novgorod, lit up yellow against a purple haze. Cars span around the junction, veering off along the Sinopskaya Riverside towards Smolny, the outer Perevozny suburbs, or back along Nevsky into the city past the Moscow railway station. The girl's hand was a stone-cold pebble in his palm. She took him halfway down a small side-street and stopped in front of a tunnel. He could taste the dampness coming off the moss-covered walls and putrescent puddles. Silence entombed them. A streetlight burned bright to one side of the bleak entrance as the iron gateway scratched a well-rutted groove. Then his guide took him out of the light, disappearing into a landscape of empty echoes.

In a small, cramped room at the top of a wooden staircase, she lay naked, long sleek legs akimbo, while Tom wrestled with his clothes in front of her. She reached out, picking up a packet of condoms, tossing them towards him.

'You must use', she ordered. He watched as she drew her knees up to her chin, revealing her innermost self to him, proffering temptation on the bedsheet. As he fumbled with the foil, she teased him in a jaded monotone. 'I want you now, you crazy boy.'

'I want you, too!' he replied, peeling off his socks, balanced awkwardly on one foot, forcing a condom over his erection. Behind him, the city lights cut through the venetian blinds, beams refracting like orange tracer shot bouncing off her bony body. He knelt over her and she opened her knees to receive him. His stomach bucked against her stretched pelvis as they moved together like rowers in a river race.

'Wait', she breathed. 'Condom is gone.'

'What?' he moaned, pushing hard, trying to reach climax.

'Stop', she urged, trying to force him out.

'Why?'

'Condom is gone', she squirmed. Tom started moving faster, his orgasm imminent. She screamed, pushing him off. He rolled away feeling angry because he had not come and guilty that he had ignored her the first time. For a moment she sat hunched back against the headboard, fingers fishing inside her vagina. Sleek and wet, her digits reappeared, nail varnish dripping, clutching the ruptured latex. She sat bolt upright. 'Turn light on!' she insisted. He reached over, hitting the button. 'Look', she said, 'this is bad, very bad!'

'Don't you take the contraceptive pill?'

'Not pill, you idiot', she raged contemptuously, 'you give me HIV!'

'No, I'm clean', he said. 'Are you?'

'Who knows? I fuck. Fucking gives illness. Condoms stop

disease. That is why you should always wear this!' She held the drooping protective between her thumb and forefinger. 'Do you think this is a turn-on? AIDS kill my friends, many friends . . .'

***

The concierge passed Tom a message straight after breakfast in the Borsalino bar. It seemed some people were waiting for him at reception. He sipped his americano and agreed for them to join him. Soon, he was sitting opposite two serious-looking characters observing him through narrow, suspicious eyes. Arkady was wearing an expensive Z-Zegna wool-mix suit. The bull-necked Bogdan, even larger-framed than the muscular Arkady, was bursting out of his jacket, his head shaved, nodding in open challenge.

'I am glad you agreed to speak with us', Arkady began, almost respectfully.

'Not at all, I always try to make myself available. How can I be of assistance?' The two Russians gave each other knowing looks as the girl returned with two white pots and cups to match. They waited a few moments, making small talk about the weather.

'You see', Arkady started to say, 'we do not generally have a high regard for your country. Maybe you will be different, I can hope so?'

Tom raised an eyebrow. 'Gentlemen, you intrigue me . . .'

'We think you are better', Bogdan chipped in incoherently.

'Better than what?'

'Grigori's Belarussian friends like Alexey Dzermant and Dmitry Dyomushin's Soyuz lunatics!'

'In what way, better?' Tom began to sound defensive. Bogdan's mouth was spitting tea.

'Well, our people don't want anybody like the National Democratic Party to succeed. We don't agree with *Rossiya, Rossiya, Rossiya, messiya gryadushchevko dny*a.' Tom's eyes widened. Arkady translated, 'O Russia, the messiah of the coming day'. Then, adding, 'In fact we hold opposing views and would prefer if the conference was boycotted!'

'What are you suggesting?'

'That you become indisposed.'

'You don't want me to speak?'

'It is not personal, we are approaching all people scheduled to talk!'

'Well, that's alright, then', Tom laughed.

'Can I report that you will be unavailable?' The academic touched his fore-head with an index finger.

'I have never been in better health!'

'Let's hope it stays that way!' Arkady said, levering himself out of the booth. 'The hospitals here have poor survival rates!'

* ❖ Production of Mebendazola is increased ten-fold to offset the growing prevalence of Central Asian diseases like ascariasis and entrebiasis;
* ❖ Outbreaks of Urban Cutaneous leishmaniasis, ethinococcis, and toxocarciasis are reported to have crossed from the *Stans* into Rostov Oblast;
* ❖ Zoonotic parasitic infections and vector-borne protozoan infections become common in Svetlograd, Novopavlovsk, and Ipatovo;
* ❖ Multiple deaths from Middle East respiratory syndrome occur in Kalmykia.

He met Ekaterina standing on the quayside in front of the Winter Palace. Her hair hung wet, gusting in the wind, flecks of corn blowing against a gun-metal sky. The high pitched cries of piebald gulls pierced the cloud line. She took him by the hand, and he used the opportunity to kiss her cheek respectfully before walking down a clanking iron footbridge onto a small motor-launch. Ekaterina haggled with the captain before Tom handed over a 500 rouble note, and they stepped onto the oil-stained decking.

The Neva travelled as far as the eye could see. To the

west was the Gulf of Finland. To the east, Archangel and
the Barents Sea. The sky welded the iron span of bridges,
structures straining to make each shoreline. Steel and
stone shoulders broke under the oppressive weight of infinite grey. Passengers gathered below a cream awning,
watching the propeller twist into action, arcing white water edging the vessel out into the brown river. Ekaterina
pointed to a flight of wildfowl drifting over the shoreline
on the Petrograd side as the pounding of a canon's me-
chanical recoil echoed from the fortress.

She explained how the Neva's origins lay in the far
north and how Lake Ladoga's frozen surface cracked in
May, sending ice floes down the full length of the river,
finally dissipating into open sea. Salty marsh islands crys-
tallised at its mouth, and lowland swamps formed which
would often be submerged beneath the swelling water.
Here, millennia before, the Izhora people had settled, and
legend had it that Prince Rurik built a stronghold at Novgorod and Prince Oleg struck out for Kiev to found a new
state. Hence, the great Varangian trade route from the
Viking Baltic to the Black Sea was born and the Neva was
its life source.

To the west, Kastelholm stood like a proud master over
the Alands. The castle's walls marked the borderlands between Finland and Tsarist Russia. From Kattegat to St Petersburg, the southern shore was mined for amber, the
legacy of the resins deposited by the ancient Lake Ancy-
lus, which drained away to form the gravel beds that were
later to mould rivers like the Vistula and the Bug. These
treacherous lagoons and fenlands proved death traps for
the Teutonic Knights as they waged their northern cru-
sades around Riga. Even today, the dark sentinels of the
Karnan and Kronborg strongholds still stood out sharply
against the dark cliff faces that dropped suddenly into the
sea.

'Kronborg was built to defend Helsingor on the Danish
side', Ekaterina was saying as if this may interest her
guest. When he shook his head dumbly, she laughed.

'English called it Elsinore. You must know Shakespeare's Hamlet?' Now it was his turn to laugh.

'I have forgotten my classes.'

Moving on up the river was like travelling back in time. He imagined an empty stream, a great silence, an impenetrable larch and pine forest. Round-topped wooden huts sat on the indented shore and salted fish hung from poles. His mind was full of tribal people like the Sami, Setus, and Karelians fighting over the best hunting grounds and farmland. The warlike Aesti gave ground to the Viking surge which followed the collapse of Rome's western empire. Their dragon prows drew east to the Black and Caspian seas.

Salt air tingled nostrils. There was no joy in the winter sunshine, just the chorus of sea birds to mark their passage. You could still smell the sweat of the serf labourers digging the foundations of the Peterhof, toiling through the mud and soil, backs breaking under the overseer's whip. In the distance, long stretches of waterway ran on ahead like a stained-glass highway. They were staring into the reflected images of domes and spires, lost in rippling tides. On silver-grey sandbanks, dead rats and effluent lay side by side. The water flowed through and past them, washing away memories, thought of time, and any sense of space. Long ago, the Swedes under Jarl Magnusson, Catholic Germans, and the Hanse merchants had navigated these stretches. All were seduced by the power of the river. Women were beguiled and men bewitched by its meandering rhythms.

In midstream, the captain nodded to the crew from the small cabin, and they began serving platters of *zakuski*. This consisted of smoked sturgeon, garlic sausage, potatoes, and mushrooms in sour cream. Tom and Ekaterina were offered chilled shots of vodka. He toasted their meeting.

'To our voyage of discovery.' The cabbage pies were unlike anything he had ever encountered. Ekaterina was eating enthusiastically. 'This is *domashni piroshki*, you say homemade.' They were looking intently into each other's eyes. 'The water always gives me an appetite', she smiled, 'You like?'

'It's all the fresh air and the smell of the wind.' She offered a salted herring on the end of a fork. He declined with a shrug of the shoulders. 'I've got enough, thanks.'

They watched as a lone woman walked down to the shoreline on the Petrograd embankment. Ekaterina waved, and the distant figure returned the compliment with a lazy, slow jerk of the arm. It seemed to Tom that it was almost an involuntary reflex response. St Petersburgers, unlike Muscovites, were naturally more communal. Regardless of their state of mind or how busy they were, their inclination was always to be more civil than those from the capital. Perhaps it was because the inhabitants had faced such barbarism, either from their own rulers, or invaders who targeted the city and singled out its people for special attention.

She told him how 300 years before, Peter the Great had planted his seed here. He was the illegitimate offspring of old Russia and the European Enlightenment. It was a new Russia of majestic palaces, lamp-lit streets, and a regulated police force. There were refuse collections and a strong sense of civic pride. Residents living near the river were punished for polluting the waterways and taxes were levied to fund municipal services. Gone were the days when bears and wolves roamed free, but savage dog packs were still common. With the flesh around their snarling muzzles drawn back, fangs dripping saliva, they attacked tourists on the streets. It was certainly wild, but in a different way than the 'time of troubles' centuries before. Then a priest blundering on the black ice, frowning under his flapping cowl, would hold his arm aloft, crude wooden crucifix in hand, exorcising the bleak soul at the heart of this pagan wilderness. The locals had long forgotten the Lion of the North, Gustavus Adolphus, but under the surface, the past still flourished. Nature-worship and Piasts fought for supremacy. The primitive still lingered.

Along the embankment, scores of couples walked hand -in-hand. The Professor felt that if he had been looking at the scene from the deck of a merchant's skiff 200 years earlier that his eyes would have witnessed a similar performance. The blue and yellow ensigns of Swedish brigantines were long gone. This was Russia's Paris now. A city of passion, mystery, and deep-seated romanticism, but still forever a stranger in its homeland.

The captain cut the engine, letting the boat drift so as not to disturb the fishermen casting out from the river's edge. Tom watched the slow, gentle flight of lines fire out in the thin light, reels whirring, the plop of lead weights taking the hook below the surface. Then the engine started up again and they went on into the great grey silence, along empty reaches, around still bends, between the high walls of tall buildings, with only the sounds of the motor to soundtrack their progress. Stone upon stone, millions of them, massive, immense iconic structures towered as they pulled through the narrow canals. The metal screw turned, churning mud-coloured waves, sending them crashing headlong into the embankment. Flapping birds trailed the boat, calling for scraps.

The vessel was aiming for the yawning mouth of the Fontanka Canal. The Summer Gardens came into view, the ornamental grille railings framing a giant vase rising out of the trees and hedges. Before them, the intricately decorated Summer Palace stood proud, looming over a tea house. 'Trezzini built this in 1712', she was saying. 'Peter the Great died here in 1725.'

'The park is beautiful.'

'Many writers liked to walk here, Taras Shevchenko, Zhukovsky, Gogol, and Alexander Blok.'

'I once visited the Taras Shevchenko University in Kiev, where Darius Stoyan studied', Tom said.

'You have been to Kiev?' Her eyes flashed. There was a hint of jealousy in her voice.

'Twice, actually. The first time I was invited to give a

memorial lecture for a man called David Lane. The second time I was presenting on Western perceptions of the politics of Ivan Franko, Vasyl Stus, and Dymtro Pavlychko.'

'I would love to visit this city', Ekaterina gasped. Then, 'If I remember correctly Franko wrote *Beyond the Limits of the Possible*?'

'Yes, indeed. My favourite line is: "anything that goes beyond the frame of the nation is hypocrisy from people of internationalised ideals which serve to provide for ethnic domination of one nation over another . . . ."'

'It's like a prediction', she replied.

'Certainly is.'

Their eyes were drawn to the sculptures of Cupid and Psyche, then the scoured marble representations of the Roman Emperor Claudius, his wife Agrippina, and her mad son Nero. Tom was wondering how many demagogues had fiddled while this megalopolis burned under incendiary attack. Leaning on the metal railings, they watched the boat swing to port side and enter the Moika. They chugged past the Swan Canal and Mikhailovsky Castle, where one paranoid Tsar was strangled to death in his own bedchamber.

Gliding around the curves under steep concrete canal walls, they advanced below the Police Bridge. Above and all around, people moved to and fro, bodies swaying, laughing, lighting cigarettes on coffee breaks from the office. Young men stood arm-in-arm with their girlfriends. Old lovers escaped the watchful eyes of neighbours, illicitly meeting among the tangle of iron and jagged masonry. Here in the heart of the city, the pulse of life was strong and fertile. You could buy anything at a price. The menu was wide open, deals were made, and transactions done quickly. This was no place for hesitation or uncertainty, it diminished credibility. Everything was about respect and the ability to pay your way. In the very cradle of Communism, money was king again. The cycle was turning, repeating itself with the inevitability of the Sun's rise and set, the Moon's waxing, and begging bowls in Africa.

Ekaterina moved closer to him. 'It is cold', she said, pulling his arm around her shoulder. Tom could smell the sweet perfume she had used to entice him. He could feel the loose strands of her hair blow against his face. He caught himself looking at her profile, waiting on her every word. His eyes watered with what he passed off as the effect of the abrasive easterly, but was really the rise of intoxicating feelings that had lain dormant far too long.

They disembarked by the Palace Bridge and stood by the Vasily Zhukovsky, Ekaterina posing modishly on the pavement, her finger jutting out to attract a passing car. Several very new European models drove on.

'I would love a ride in that', Tom indicated as an Audi sports car swung away from them.

'They do not need our money, they have enough of their own.' Eventually, a beaten-up VW pulled over, leaking oil and puffing fumes. The asthmatic driver wore a cloth cap and toothless grin, and cast an otherworldly gaze over them. Ekaterina leaned in close to negotiate a price. '*Skolka?*' Tom watched her step back from the man's toxic breath. Then, tugging on the door, she turned, telling him to get in. The Professor sat amid a collection of discarded pizza boxes and sardine-smeared overhauls, listening as Ekaterina gave slow and simple directions.

They entered Nevsky from the Neva end, travelling as far as the Kazan cathedral, before the dark sky broke and bright sunshine covered the thoroughfare. 'Look', Ekaterina said excitedly, dropping her usually reserved demeanour and pointing upwards. 'It is a rainbow, you must make a wish!' Tom could see the variegated light painting the brimstone colonnades of the cathedral. The vibrant red, yellow, and violet were made all the clearer set against the crisp arctic air.

'Make wish!' she encouraged.

'I already did', he said, reaching forward to squeeze her shoulder.

'And you will not tell me what you prayed for?'

'No, of course not. That would spoil the surprise.'

The driver shot Tom a mean glance through the rear-
view, pulling over, talking harshly as Ekaterina thrust
money at him, notes cascading between thin legs. Tom
almost fell out through the door as the car accelerated
away. Halfway across the road, he grabbed her by the arm.
'What was that all about?' At first she did not answer. He
saw a look of discomfort distort her youthful features, but
he was genuinely curious and not a little angry, so he per-
sisted with his questions. Stopping to avoid the oncoming
traffic, she looked deep into his face, evaluating how he
would respond to what she told him.

'He said I was selling myself to a Westerner and should
find myself a good Russian man for marriage.' Their fingers interlocked.

'Then good Russian men will have to wait in line.'

Following a drink in the Sea Bell, they parted temporarily on the eastern side of Nevsky. He trailed back to his
room to await their rendezvous in the foyer of the An-
gleterre. The arms of the giant clock on the former KGB
building at the corner of Bolshaya Morskaya read 13.15.
Occasionally, a sunbeam would fall through the cloud
cover, alighting on a spiral cone of flies hovering over an
open restaurant vent. The waft of sour cabbage followed
him. To either side, the colossal buildings pressed in. He
had a sense of what it must have felt like to be one of
those comical clerks Gogol had written so eloquently
about: insignificant biological entities with big noses and
frayed overcoats playing out their meaningless lives in this
vast metropolis of oblong architecture. His stride length-
ened and he puffed out his chest, trying to maximise his
proportions in response to his surroundings. Somehow,
the designers of this interminable city had found a way to
crush the individual will whilst instilling in the collective a
subconscious civic dignity. It was a truly marvellous psy-
chological achievement which had served the rulers well,
regardless of their political alignment. He could see those
familiar red eyelids over the arched windows ahead. His
mind was on the girl. She was intriguing him. What had

Churchill said about Russia? 'A riddle, wrapped in a mystery, inside an enigma', or something like that.

- ❖ People are herded into Kazan's sixteenth-century Annunciation Cathedral and burnt to death in the shadows of the Spasskaya Tower. The President of Tartarstan, speaking from the Qol-Sarif Mosque, described the action as 'defensive';
- ❖ A second Battle of the Torches takes place on the slopes of the Tabasaran Mountains, with the insurgents achieving their objective in cutting the railway to the south towards Baku and seizing the road to Rostov-on-Don;
- ❖ During the second Tokhtamysh-Timur skirmish, the Bolghar complex is captured and turned into a centre for a local *hajj* for the Muslim population;
- ❖ The Astrakhan Kremlin's Maria Ascension Cathedral holds a final Christian Mass prior to the forced expulsion of ethnic Russians;
- ❖ Evidence of human sacrifice in the de-consecrated Unzha Chapel is revealed on State TV. In response, Orthodox believers raise the holy icon of St Prince Mikhail of Tver and commence an armed pilgrimage to Stavropol.

5.

They cannot understand as yet that we are not
fighting a political party, but a sect of murderers of
all contemporary spiritual culture.—Baron Roman
von Ungern-Sternberg

When he got back to the hotel, Ulrich Hoffman was at
reception, getting ready to check out. Whirling creases
surrounding deep-set eyes emphasised the intensity with
which he was scrutinising the computer printout spilling
from the till. Tom's sudden appearance, however, caught
the German's attention.

'One moment', Hoffman said as he signed off the receipt and collected his American Express card. 'Do you
have time to talk?' There was a paternal look on the veteran's face.

'Not really.' Tom felt surly, contemptuous of Hoffman's
apparent cowardice. He was in no mood for a condescend-
ing lecture.

'I think you do, Professor Hunter.' There was something in the tone. The German's voice was commanding
Tom to listen. 'Come with me.'

They walked in silence out of the lobby and across the
square. Ten minutes later, somewhere in the backstreets
on the Neva side of the Marinskii, Hoffman led him into a
small courtyard. They walked up some steps. A narrow
path rose directly to the doors of a synagogue. The place
was open, a portal to another world. 'We will not be dis-
turbed here.' Tom sensed his companion was trying to
sound protective, not pressurising. Pigeons flapped over
gravestones. Pale Hasidic Jews in black yarmulkes sauntered between the monuments, talking animatedly to each

other.

'Look', Tom began, 'what is all this?'

Ulrich tried not to look offended. 'Carl Jung once said, "The Jew who is something of a nomad has never yet created a culture form of his own and as far as we can see never will, since all his instincts and talents require a more or less civilised nation to act as host for their development".'

'You're beginning to sound like Ezra Pound. Wasn't it he who insisted we should keep Jews out of banking, education, and government?'

'It served the Byzantines well, the longest-lasting empire in the history of the world.'

'But we live in the post-Enlightenment.'

'So we do, and Bolshevism was the bastard child of that deeply optimistic, utopian ideal: the classless society that supposedly transcends conflict and economic exploitation. The sort of nonsense that resulted in the pseudo-science of Trofim Lysenko and the prison colonies of Karaganda.'

'So what are you going to do?'

'Ms Karre has already left for the airport!'

'So?'

'You may want to consider following her example.'

'Why?'

'Threats! Our friends in the Bloc use some very unsound methods!'

Tom shook his head. 'So you are running? Grigori's people can protect us!'

'They are not so well-organised or so well-connected to the underworld. Have you been contacted?'

'Yes, they threatened me also, but I told them . . .'

'You don't have a family?' the older man's irascible voice advised. 'Leave now like the rest of us. Grigori is organising a counter-demonstration. There will be a war and we will be responsible.'

'You saw how our Dutch friend handled them the other day!'

'He's one man, for God's sake!'

'You said Grigori's bringing our people out in force. And of course there are the police.'

'My previous experience with the Russian authorities does not fill me with great confidence.'

'I see . . .'

'Do you, really? Let me tell you a little story in keeping with a place like this.' He waved towards the sacred stones. 'There was a rabbi called Loew who poured spring water on some mountain soil. He walked around this pile of earth singing incantations and reciting from ancient scriptures, "Ata Bra Golem Dewuk Hachomer W' tigzar Zedim Chewel Torfe Jisrael", and a life was formed, a Golem. A creature that did its master's bidding. And its master inserted a *shem* into its mouth so that he always had complete control over its thought and actions.'

'You speak in parables.'

'The Golem is like a robot.'

'So?'

'The Bloc is an army of Golems!'

***

They met over a glass of Courvoisier in the Borsalino before tilting umbrellas against the storm slewing across Palace Square. Navigating gusty arches, they entered the Hermitage's inner courtyard, fork lightning slicing through sulphurous smog. Then, waiting with some Italian tourists to check their coats and bags, they marched hand-in-hand past security, old men with jaundiced expressions ripe for reliquaries.

Mounting the Jordan staircase, looking skywards at gilt stucco and classical statues, they watched as a mesmeric shimmer of light played across gold and white. Stone faces transformed into ghostly apparitions, arms and shoulders cut from the purest marble overseeing a staircase lit by crystal chandeliers. He was enchanted by the wood carvings on the doors, entering endless galleries filled with Rembrandts, Van Dycks, Monets, and Picassos. Whole rooms were given over to Sassanid gemstones and ancient Scythian hoards. A labyrinth of panelling led from one treasure to another. Great, sky-lit windows cast grey, powdery light down into the vaults. A thousand Ali Baba caves collected together. Sculptures, ceremonial swords, Stone Age artefacts, and Egyptian mummies piled up in every corner.

They paused at Raphael's *The Madonna Conestabil.* He was struck by how the face in the painting resembled the woman standing next to him.

'We were taught in school that art had a hierarchy', Ekaterina was whispering in his ear. 'First, there were the fine arts, then minor arts, then civilised art, and barbaric art. Painters were the same. Raphael's beauty was superior to Da Vinci's depth or Michelangelo's form and texture. This is an early Raphael. He learned his trade in Perugino's studio in Urbino.'

Tom's eyes flowed over the blue cloak, pink neck, and red dress clasped over delicate breasts. 'It is very beautiful.'

'Pergino's Madonna sequence greatly influenced Raphael's work. There is no artifice, it is almost perfectly innocent, don't you agree?'

'Oh yes, most certainly.' But Tom could not tear himself away from the face, a reflection of Ekaterina caught on canvas.

In the Chinese gallery, while she stood entranced before a fourteenth century silk tapestry, they met two friends who had been amongst the crowd at Marina's the night before. After a few minutes of excited chatter, drawing disparaging remarks from uniformed attendants, Ekaterina asked if the young men would like to join Tom and her in the Persian rooms before getting a coffee and a bite to eat.

Yuri was an arts graduate with a warm, intelligent disposition. He wore a sheepskin coat and cowboy boots. His conversation was littered with references to poems by Constantin von Hoffmeister as he lit cigarette after cigarette and stirred sugar after sugar into his cup. Alexei was younger, still studying philosophy, pale and acne-riddled, his manners refined, almost effeminate, his voice light like a piccolo.

'You have wonderful theatres and museums', Tom said, throwing up his arms, opening them wide, trying to en-compass the whole twenty kilometres of corridors and rooms above their heads.

'But for how long?' Alexei questioned, 'We are under siege just like before. You know, in the Great Patriotic War the chief conservator here stockpiled crates and straw to protect everything. The staff would fetch and car-ry along the corridors and galleries for hours and hours, even during the German bombardment.' Tom's imagina-tion was fired by spiralling lights cascading over the Neva, anti-aircraft fire pounding along the embankment, tracer shells like fireworks in the night. 'Trucks were loaded and armed convoys took the artefacts away down the Nevsky towards the railway station. I think they smuggled out millions of items right under the noses of the fascist Tiger tanks.'

'And those times have returned?' Yuri shook the ash from his Marlboro.

'Worse. At least the Nazis were cultured. Now we are besieged by *svoloch.*' Alexei went on.

'They broke up the Mad Crowd Gang, killing Dmitry Borovikov and arresting Ruslan Melnik.'

'The ones who allegedly murdered the anti-fascist campaigner Nikolai Girenko?'

'Girenko was pro-African. Did you read *Novy Peters-burg*: "It's obvious that these black-skinned Africans are coming to our country from stagnant places that are teeming with infections. Bacteria and microbes living in Africa represent a serious danger to the health of White people." Just look at the outbreaks of tuberculosis in your own country, the viruses sweeping France. Girenko was a tool of the Sova Centre, acting against us.'

'The us, being?'

'Russky Obraz, Shultz 88, and Russian Republic!'

'And Alexei Voyevodin and Artyom Prokhorenko?'

'Heroes!'

'But those not dead are in prison.'

'Look, the cops were under orders. Putin was hosting big international meetings both here and in Moscow. But not all the cops are bad, many are on our side. Some, though, are like Kolovrat says: They do not have nationality or fatherland, Zionists turned them into house dogs".'

'He's right', Alexei chimed in. 'Many have sympathy for the Boevaga Organisation Russkih Natssionalistov, some are even in our combat units.'

'I've read that Nikita Tikhonov and Yevgenia Khasis were in contact with Leonid Simulin, one of Vladislav Surkov's operatives.'

'I was there when they were sentenced for executing that dog Markelov. They were holding hands, how you say, dignified.'

'And Russky Verdikt continues to appeal for their release.'

'But of course, there are many unanswered questions about that Moscow trial. We all know they were acting on orders from the top when Nikita fired the Browning pistol into that human rights activist's head.'

'Do you think they killed the anti-fascist militant Khutorsky?'

'Someone did.'

'And could you guys kill?'

'Hell, yes, but we'll only kill for Utro Rossii!'

'Dawn of Russia', Ekaterina interpreted. Tom nodded, knowing of the rise of the paramilitary group, similar to that of the Resistance in France.

For a time they sat in silence. Yuri stubbed his cigarette, Alexei bit into a sandwich. Ekaterina sipped her cappuccino.

'Listen', Yuri eventually said, 'if you want to see what it is really like, come to my place. I've got a movie called *Russia 88.*'

'That's banned, right?'
'Not at my place!'

They trudged past shuttered shop fronts and court-yards full of broken furniture, walking shattered streets littered with condoms and silver foil. Confronted by a sudden hole in the road, they skirted the web of rusted pipes feeding the apartment blocks, hissing steam and spitting vapour, noxious sulphur rising into the air.

Alexei caught the incredulous look on Tom's face. 'So much for communal services', he explained. 'It's worse now than the Gorbachev time!'

'Look, I was born here', declared Yuri. 'They built kindergartens next to factories. Can you imagine all this filth being breathed by kids? Alexei, on his case comes from Vyborg.'

'Yes, Lenin's land, they called me the Finn at college.'

'And other things too!' The two exchanged angry smiles. Ekaterina remained silent, walking arm-in-arm with Tom, picking their way through detritus.

They entered a mouldering entranceway, climbing staircases covered in anarchist graffiti. Curling As at the centre of swirling crimson circles had taken over from swastikas and the hammer and sickle. A fat rat waddled by, glass claws scurrying over tiles. Ekaterina screamed, jumping backwards. 'Looks like they're laying poison again', Alexei said, pointing to the creature's cannibalised companion, a tangle of ripped fur and warm blood.

Yuri's flat was at the top of the block. Drafty and dark, a single lightbulb lit a faded poster of Spartak Moscow's former Miss Charming, Olga Kuzkova, as they took seats around a low table and Alexei slopped vodka into freshly-rinsed glasses. 'A toast', he insisted. 'To broadening cultural horizons!'

Yuri went to a cupboard and rooted around amongst the clutter, tossing Arkona CDs, flashcards filled with live performances by Solncevorot, and books by Louis Pauwels and Hermann Wirth aside. Meanwhile, Tom was going through his host's back copies of radical journals: *Russkoe Vremia, Elementy, Istoki,* and *Milyi Angel*. 'Here it is!' Yuri declared triumphantly, 'starring Pyotr Fyodorov, Kabez Kibizov, Aleksandr Makarov, and Vera Strokova.' He was laughing. 'I bet you never heard of them, right?'

'They are pretty unfamiliar, I have to admit', Tom was forced to confess. 'Can I take a look?' He reached out for the plastic box. The scratched cover read in English, 'A cross between *Romper Stomper* and *This is England*'. Obviously an imported pirate copy. The photograph gave him no clue as to the identities of the actors. 'Gangland?' he surmised.

'A *skazka*', Yuri's eyes glistened. 'A fairy tale of Moscow!'

Alexei inserted the disc and hit play. For the next two hours the room was filled with skinheads. Their leader, Sasha, known as Blade, was a role model for his young companions. 'We want to be partisans like Sabine and Luc in France', Yuri admitted.

'A regular Bonnie and Clyde', said Tom, adding, 'Or Butch Cassidy and the Sundance Kid.' They had never heard of either outlaw duo. It made him feel old. He was wondering if he could ever connect with these people. Sure, they were laughing, but was it with him or at him? He could not tell.

Later, they drank more vodka and talked politics. Yuri was very active in the pagan underground. 'Vulcari!' Ekaterina explained. Tom shook his head.

'What?'

'Wolf men!'

'Like Patrol 35 or the Sychev Faction!' Alexei exclaimed. He pulled out a book entitled *The Slavic Gods* by Pavel Tulaev, and passed it to Tom, who flipped through the pages, noting the depictions of legendary Rus heroes like Svarovich, Lada, Svarog, and Bereginya surrounded by runic inscriptions. Alexei was a big fan of Repin and explained in great detail the significance of folklore in works like *Sadko in the Underwater Kingdom*. 'We are all *iazy-*

cheskii natsionalizm, like animals and tribal', he said. 'It is a great shame that the Orthodox followers of Vladimir toppled the statues of Perun into the Dnieper and raised the holy cross over Kiev.' Ekaterina, listless but engaged, talked about Masha 'the scream', archaeology, and Emelyanov's paganism.

'Gladiator!' Yuri screamed, 'I have a copy on disc.' staggering to his bookcase, he waved another DVD in the air. 'This is great. Did you see the part where the legionnaire's missile cuts Herman's head right off?'

After viewing *Gladiator*, they took him to a shabby tenement on Lesnoy Prospekt to introduce him to Alyosha, the head of the local Vulcari. The White Rex patrol leader stood straight-backed in a Rammstein t-shirt, hand on hip, explaining in clear English that his gym trained street fighters to take on the foreigners who were gaining ascendancy on the streets.

'Our people are ideologically sound', Alyosha said matter of factly. 'Good brains control strong muscle!'

'And your coaches?' Tom asked as they entered the fitness room to the sound of Molodyozh Tule.

'Most are ex-army.' then, pointing towards a square-shouldered guy in a green vest, 'Dimitra is currently serving!'

'Reliable, then?'

'Very. But we also have international specialists to help us.'

'Really?'

'Yes, we have a very good guy called Piter Janssen.'

'I've met him. How good is he?'

'They say he is the best!'

Tom acknowledged a mixed group of trainees, gathering about them. 'New recruits?'

'Just last week', Alyosha confirmed.

'They look fit', the Professor mused out loud as his eyes fixed on a girl in khaki shorts and a crop top, pounding a punchbag.

'Saniya is a Masters student at the Finance and Economics University.'

'I wouldn't want to fight her', Tom breathed.

'Don't!' Alexei warned from behind. 'She floored me yesterday with one kick!'

Alyosha sat down with his guests under a double-headed eagle flag.

'The situation here is becoming critical', he admitted. 'Survival skills will be vital in the future. The Tajiks, Turkmen, and Uzbeks are everywhere. Muslim gangs run the drugs and the girls. They don't hesitate to kill and neither should we!'

'And the military?'

'Mixed experience', Alyosha said sardonically. 'Some, of course, are sympathetic, others, like the cops, can be bought.'

'But at least political correctness is weak here. You are freer than us to push back.'

'Yes', Alyosha laughed. 'I have seen how your rulers impose laws that mean you cannot fight. It is crazy!'

'Such pain is self-imposed.' The Russian shook his head.

'We will have none of that shit here!'

'So I see.'

'Our patrol is very united', Alyosha insisted. 'Alexei and Yuri will tell you. Close physical contact creates deep bonds and weapons training builds confidence.' At that point he slipped an OTS-38 revolver out of his combat trousers and released the safety. 'We will fight to the finish.'

When Tom returned to the Astoria, a receptionist thrust a bundle of messages into his hands. His telephone was jammed with incoming calls, a little red light winking in the darkness. He bent down to pick up a calling card that had been slipped under his door. It read *Tom Hunter RIP*.

Sitting on the corner of his bed, he flicked through the

concierge's hand-written notes. One was a coded message from the League of St George in London requesting his immediate return. He knew it must be important so picked up his mobile phone and keyed a response. His head was full of the girl. Her ever-changing expression, the way she paid attention as he spoke.

He kicked off his shoes, pondering the text reply he subsequently received from the UK, lying silent for many hours. Outside, a damask shroud hung over St Isaacs. Glass in hand, he was weighing up his options. Staying and speaking was certainly risky. But it also gave him the chance to make his name. He would also be furthering the Russian cause and show support for the intellects of Evraziiskoe obozrenie. He pondered the odds of him making a difference and why after all these years of emotionless sex this young woman should appear on the scene, just when he needed a clear head? He poured himself another scotch, swirled the ice, and took a deep, satisfying gulp. The hours passed.

A pale sun rose over the eastern shoulder of the Dome, the Cathedral's heavy head propped on granite forearms. Tom caught hold of the curtains. His mind drifting, he had been dreaming about Yesenin slashing his wrists, composing those last verses in his own blood. The Professor rolled off the bed, wandering into the bathroom. Looking at his face in the mirror, it struck him as particularly vulnerable and forlorn. He was in in need of a strong shot of coffee. Splashing cold water on opaque eyes, he looked over his shoulder, feeling self-disgust at the sight of discarded clothes and soiled tissues strewn on the carpet.

**

Ekaterina woke and almost immediately asked herself why she was so interested in this man? He was not especially good looking, nor rich. Turning over on the pillow she pondered, I am a modern woman, I can do whatever I desire. So what if he was old enough to be her father? What if he was a foreigner? His politics attracted her. His intellect drew her like a moth to the flame.

Leaping out of bed and taking a shower, she looked at her narrow waist and long legs. She touched her breasts and the dark triangle between her legs. His face was in her mind, his aftershave in her nostrils. Afterwards she towelled herself dry, fixed her hair, and pulled on her panties. Standing bare-breasted in front of the mirror, she applied a little make up, not so much that it looked like she was trying, but just enough to add some haphazard elegance. The world around her began to wake. First, the familiar door slammed, then the radio stations broke that morning's news:

- ❖ Teip head-hunting clans tighten their grip on the former Soviet-Orient, characterised by patronage and nepotism on a colossal scale;
- ❖ The rate of extraction of hydrocarbons in Central Asia escalates to feed unprecedented growth in the Chinese economy;
- ❖ Immigrant shanty towns spring up around Suzdal's Golden Ring, Kostroma, and Myshkin. The M8 motorway is log-jammed by carts and wagons rolling westwards;
- ❖ At the Kotorosi River crossing in Yaroslavl Utro Rossii, militants clash with armed immigrants ransacking districts on the east bank;
- ❖ The Kozelshchina icon is seized and destroyed by as yet unspecified people in Poltava.

Ekaterina fastened her trousers, slid on shoes, stirred and drank instant coffee. She watched as a silver ripple of condensation ran down the window. Outside, birds swooped, flocking to catch the breadcrumbs old Mrs Kozlov cast from her balcony.

Swinging on her coat, Ekaterina made to leave, eager to make their rendezvous at the Blue Bridge. The door rattled in its warped frame. Twisting the key in the latch, a double lock mechanism clicked inside. Then, the sound of her footsteps carried up through the cavernous stairwell, as her shoes tap-danced to the street.

Ten minutes later they were walking over the Sinny Most, making towards the Yusupov Palace, which sat shrouded in spectral mystery on the bank of the Moika. She was thinking that Tom looked great, his face shaved and flinty in the morning light. His body was tall and firm inside his long black coat. There was something unique about him, she thought. Something she could not resist.

They were talking about history and philosophy, arguing over the merits of Kierkegaard's *Fear and Loathing* and Knut Hamsun's *Growth of the Soil.*

'It's good we debate', she said. 'It is a sign of a healthy relationship.' A white coach with Swedish registration plates sat opposite the palace on the rain raddled road.

Starry-eyed with scurrilous rumour, Ekaterina related, 'The Yusupov's were one of the richest families in St Petersburg. Felix, Rasputin's killer was a well-known homosexual. It is said that he was a most beautiful man, married to the Princess Irina, the Tsar's niece . . .' She paused, pushing on the door to number 94. 'He had been to England, educated at Oxford. There were stories that he had won the heart of a Duke's daughter, but when he returned home there was disapproval of the match with Irina because of his predilections. Being gay was punishable by exile. Some historians even say there may have been strong love feelings between Yusupov and Rasputin.'

'I thought Rasputin was a ladies' man?'

A wicked smile passed over her face, reading the signs, checking the entry price. 'He was, how you say, bi-curious too!'

They bought tickets for 300 roubles, then gathered with some Americans and Scandinavians at the foot of a marble staircase. Chandeliers swung on the roof above as they followed the guide up the red carpet, turning to look back down into the vast lobby.

Professorial in demeanour, with white hair knotted in a tight, spinster-like fist at the back of her small head, the interlocutor struck a pose of relaxed authority, coughing loudly to gain their attention.

'300,000 people visit the palace every year.' Her arm extended as if to embrace the entrance. 'It is renowned for its furnishings, art, and of course the assassination of Father Gregory, more commonly known as Rasputin, confidante of the Tsarina in the last years before the Revolution.'

They were taken through drawing rooms, bedrooms, and a ballroom with shining mirrors and classical motifs. Ekaterina lingered over the pastoral scenes in the glass-plated long gallery, while Tom was captivated by the waxwork representations of the conspirators on that fateful night of December 29. He tried to picture Madeira cakes laced with potassium cyanide. The sound of 'Yankee Doodle Dandy' spinning out of the gramophone in a desperate attempt to make it sound like a party was going on in the rooms above. Meanwhile Rasputin, the *Starets*, was led like Isaac by his father Abraham into the basement room below, ready for slaughter.

Just before eleven, the tourists descended a flight of stairs into a private theatre. The walls were decorated in a sumptuous mixture of orange, white, and gold. On the ceiling was a gaudy fresco, and over Tom's left shoulder a private box from where the Romanovs and Yusupovs sat in the dying days of the Empire.

Tom looked out onto a derelict garden veiled in smog, a small metal gate lying at the southern entrance. He tried to picture the scene. Rasputin staggering out of a side door, bleeding from a bullet in his chest. His executioners rushing out into the moonlight after him. Revolvers sparking in the dark before a single bullet struck him in the back. Then, the British secret serviceman stepping out of the shadows to deliver the *coup de grace* at point-blank range.

The guide's words rang loudly in Tom's mind. 'Quoting Gregory Yemfimovich Rasputin', she declaimed, '"If I am killed by common assassins . . . especially peasants, the Tsar and his children would have nothing to fear and would reign for hundreds of years. But if I am murdered by nobles, then none of the Tsar's children or relations will remain alive for more than two years, they will be killed by the Russian people . . ."'

How prophetic, he thought. Perhaps there was more to this dark force of nature who could cure haemophiliacs and seduce society ladies. The British were right to kill him before he persuaded the Tsarina to advise her husband to withdraw the Imperial forces from the Eastern Front, freeing the Germans to sweep both the French and His Britannic Majesty's armies into the Channel.

What these conspirators could not have known was the seventy years of Communist rule that would fill the power vacuum, after the bayonets and bullets had done their work in Ekaterinburg. Now that was ironic. In killing off a troublesome priest, they had stirred up a whirlwind that led to Stalin's purges, mud-filled gulags, and the partition of the European continent.

Tom felt the death shroud fall over his face, smelling burning flesh and tasting the gunpowder caked at the back of his throat.

'Are you OK?' Ekaterina asked, bending close to his ear, arm curling affectionately around his shoulder. 'You look troubled.'

'I'm fine, can we get a drink somewhere?' She took his hand and led him down the staircase, out onto the water's edge. An amplified voice from a tour bus that was driving along the embankment chafed the stillness like an electronic cheese grater. 'St Petersburg is called the Venice of the north. Home to . . .' And there the sound trailed out, the back of the bus disappearing behind vaporous curtains of speckled grey.

They were pressed together, arms entwined. Tom let

his mind drift. He was telling himself that this could be love, and scorned himself for thinking it. He could not recall being so moved by a woman. That drunken weekend in Singapore with the Aussie radical did not count. He had put that down to the humidity rather than loneliness.

Cars swirled around them as they strolled past a man selling fake Rolex watches from a blanket spread on the side of the road. A doe-eyed bitch snivelled and whelped, rolling onto her back, revealing milky tits to five mewling puppies. Ekaterina bent down to stroke them. The street-seller cornered Tom, opening his coat to reveal contra-band Seiko, Hugo Boss, and Cartier.

'Come on', Tom said, pulling Ekaterina to her feet, 'let's get something to eat. The merchant swore as his dog chased them down the canal bank, barking madly at their heels.

Climbing some steps to a small café, they took seats at a table with a vase of fresh-cut daisies and asters. The waitress smiled indulgently while they studied the menu. Ekaterina ordered a coffee; Tom, a dark beer, before they both decided on *ukha*, traditional fish soup. He could not be sure what music was playing in the background. Folk music, maybe. He could not tell. There was something familiar about it, a sort of militaristic nostalgia. 'Of course, *Svoi*, "Our People", sung by Lyube', he mumbled, remembering that the lacklustre middle-of-the road band was the former President's favourite group.

'You like?' she asked, pointing to the brown bottle he raised to his lips.

'Yeah', he assured her. 'It is early for me to start drinking, but I need it.'

'Problems?'

'Sort of.' Then he added, 'Sometimes people will do anything to stop the truth.'

'For some people, the truth hurts!'

Tom shrugged. 'Look, Grigori's going to raise an army to confront the Bloc.'

'I have heard the rumours.'

'Can he do it?'

Ekaterina thought carefully. 'Yes, there are many sympathisers.'

'But it will lead to a pitched battle.'

'It is the natural consequence of what you are doing.'

'What I'm doing?'

'Thinkers like you talk. Others fight!'

- ❖ The EU, UN, and USA declare the exiled Alexander Dugin a public enemy and move to seize any assets he holds in countries where they have legal jurisdiction;
- ❖ Plans to develop industrial-scale food production in the liberated zones of Ukraine are announced;
- ❖ The Qahal, the Assembly of God, meet in the reconstituted all-Jewish town of Budaniv on the banks of the Seret River in Ukraine;
- ❖ All traces of Ruthenian culture are deemed anti-Semitic and draconian sentences are imposed to end politically incorrect activities in the Carpathians.

Stepping out as a dark cowl of cloud slipped over the Cathedral's cupola, Tom was in an exuberant mood. He was telling Ekaterina about London, his life and work. They turned a blind corner, hurrying back to the Astoria, when by pure chance he caught sight of Arkady's face in a crowded black limousine on the blue bridge. Revving its engine impatiently, the occupants were locked in earnest debate, deciding who to intimidate next. Tom lowered his voice, raised his collar, and slipped his arm around Ekaterina's waist, walking on stiffly, turning his head away, trying to blend in with other pedestrians.

Despite his best efforts, Arkady spotted them, lowering the window to shout.

'English', he called. 'English!'

'Keep walking', Tom advised.

'What is it?' she asked, hearing his name being called,

surprised by the force he used to guide her away. Arkady kept calling as Tom led her across the square, twisting his neck just in time to catch sight of shaven-headed Bogdan opening the passenger door, while Arkady sped off, intending to cut them off before they could reach the Astoria.

'Keep going', Tom insisted.

'Where?'

'Away from the hotel.'

'What is wrong?'

'Those people don't like to hear the truth!'

'Our truth, you mean?'

Tom smiled confirmation.

They rushed towards Nevsky, bouncing along wood planking that had been built for commuters to bypass the construction work. Behind, moving stiffly, but with quiet determination, Bogdan followed, reaching into his pocket, ready to call Arkady on his mobile. Traffic was congested. Arkady was struggling to turn the car onto Bolshaya Morskaya when his mobile rang.

'*Da*', he said, then listening intently. '*Ublyudok!*' he spat, big knuckles drumming on the steering wheel. In the back, two other Bloc men sat in silence. 'Get out and follow', he commanded. 'Don't lose them.' The rear doors swung open, dispatching fresh attack dogs into the metropolitan centre of the former Leningrad.

Tom and Ekaterina reached Nevsky junction, turning right toward Kazan, rain lacerating them like iced grapeshot. They pushed on over the first canal bridge, looking back to see if they were still being followed. Their predators were clearly visible, wolf-like eyes intent on their prey. Bogdan was 30 metres distant, talking breathlessly into his mobile, giving directives to the foot soldiers. His stride widened as he strove to close on them. His accomplices had successfully circumnavigated the Admiralty and were now on the opposite side of Nevsky.

Poised on the curb, waiting for gaps in the hurtling headlights, Tom and Ekaterina began running, bolting between oncoming cars, slipping between the shadows cast by the Cathedral's colonnades. Consumed by narrow passages, Tom felt that familiar uneasiness which always overcame him in enclosed spaces. He was straining to keep up, thigh muscles choking on lactic acid. Torrential rain fell as Tom stopped, slumped against a wall, bracing himself, the nausea overwhelming. Ekaterina waited.

'You shouldn't have drunk so much!'

He rolled his eyes and vomited. 'I'm too old for this', he confessed to himself. Some 20 metres on, an archway gave to the left. The entrance was partially cordoned off by concrete slabs. Ekaterina handled these hurdles with relative ease, whilst he stumbled through them, heavy-legged, just making out the girl's pale features refracting in the air blowing west from the streetlights on Nevsky.

'If we go this way', she was saying, 'we go back to the street and come behind them. They will never know.' Tom nodded numbly. Ekaterina began clambering over some railings. Tom, gasping, copied her, heart thumping, spitting bile.

For a moment they stood side by side, cars chasing light snakes over the tarmac. Crossing to the eastern side of the Gribeodova to catch a lift, Arkady's black car skidded to a halt in front of them. He was hitting the horn, yelling for them to get inside, but they had already taken off down the canal bank, past the Sakura, slapping steps weaving around a growling motorbike. Bogdan and the others emerged from the crowd of onlookers and gave chase in a flurry of hats and coats.

Ekaterina grabbed Tom's damp sleeve, pulling him towards the entrance of the Church of the Saviour on Spilled Blood. Disappearing into the congregation, they joined pilgrims squeezing through the narrow doorway, shuffling into a vestibule where carved figures flew about the walls. The smell of sodden wool permeated the air. Within the candlelit sepulchre, a circle of crow-robed priests stood in silent contemplation, their beards black, cloth veils falling from their headgear. The low mutter of prayer began resonating in the gloom. Tom stared upwards, clouds of blue incense obscuring the mosaic of the Christ Pantocrator, wondering if this was a sanctuary or a gilded trap. He noted that Ekaterina's face was flushed with exertion as they approached Alexander II's shrine, self-conscious footfalls resounding on Italian marble. She slid her hand into his.

'Who were those people?'

'Bloc partisans.'

'More like *gruppirovka.*' Tom looked blank. 'Gangs!'

***

- ❖ Behind the scenes, nationalist sympathisers in the Russian High Command were taking control of the new military command structure, at strategic, operational, and brigade level;
- ❖ Vitaly Milonov, a former St Petersburg Councillor and lawmaker for Vladimir Putin, makes a return to the public sphere, advocating for the celebration of St John of Kronstadt, a man connected with the Black Hundred;
- ❖ Thousands flock to Tolyatti where Mary's icon is raised, symbolically offering protection against hostile forces;
- ❖ 'Resistance', Vitaly Averyanov, President of the Institute of Dynamic Conservatives, repeated again and again, 'is a sign of life.'

Grigori paced back and forth, eagerly awaiting the call from Federal Security headquarters in Lubyanka Square, Moscow. 'Hydra goes green', was the message. 'We are sanctioning the assassination of President Babel', a dry voice confirmed after giving the appropriate *Syny Otechestva*, Sons of the Fatherland, authentication code. 'Spetsnaz units will be deployed to assist the operation.'

'Date, time, and location?'

'Babel will be attending a dinner party organised by his fellow tribesman Mikhail Mirilashvili at a private house on

Bolshoy Prospekt tomorrow. He will take the Blagovesh-
chenskiy Most crossing, following the university embankment route and *liniya*.'

'And your men will be the same ones you used in Ma-
khachkala?'

'Yes, they are already in the city and will contact you.'

'I will tell the Dutchman to be ready.'

'Remember, it is important we have clean hands', the
Muscovite threatened.

'Do not worry', Grigori confided. 'This man was trained
by the Norwegian Forsvarets Spesialkommando.'

Then, after raising a private toast to the mission's success, he called Alyosha, pressing him for a show of
strength on the street as a diversion. 'We need everyone
out on Nevsky. Massed flags, music, and weapons. Leave
no one behind. Every man, woman and child, understand?' Alyosha agreed. 'Make sure Martsinkevich's
FAMAT 18 hard men are there, this will be war.'

'Understood!'

***

Ekaterina lived in a nineteenth-century apartment off the
Ulitsa Yakubbovicha. They went up four flights of spiral
steps with twisting banisters. Drafty French windows
opened out onto a narrow balcony with a split plinth over-
looking an inner courtyard. Throwing open the shutters,
her graphite pupils caught the starlight. 'You will be safe
here', she said confidently. 'There are no monsters.'

'Monsters?'

'What Glukhovsky calls the Dark Ones, *Homo novus*—
the next stage in evolution.'

'You like *Metro 2033*, too?'

'Of course, it is an allegory for our times. We are like
the hero Artyom battling another species. Take a look
around you; they are rising. We fooled ourselves into
thinking we had rid ourselves of the people who geno-
cided millions upon millions of real Russians after their

so-called Worker's Revolution. But we were wrong; they have returned even stronger, with new allies from the south and east. And soon, just like Wells' Morlocks, they will be hunting us in the streets.'

'You are certainly one of the Eloi', he flattered her.

They sat and talked. She was descended from an old Leningrad family, her great grandmother having attended the Smolny Institute for young noblewomen.

'Have you been active in the movement long?'

'It depends what you mean by active.'

'Meetings, marches, that kind of thing.'

'Since my early teens, I guess. Just as soon as I read Kollar's epic poem *Slavy dcera*, Slava's daughter.'

'And your friends?'

'Most, yes, but my grandfather is the most influential on me.'

'Parents?'

She went quiet and changed the subject.

The flat comprised three rooms. A cramped lounge, with an antique clock, an Afghan rug, and bookshelves filled to bursting; a dining room-cum-kitchen with a small stove and Formica table littered with pots, pans, herbs, oils, and vinaigrette; and sleeping quarters barely large enough for a double bed.

He paid particular attention to some of her own art hung over the fireplace whilst Ekaterina put on Halgrath's dark ambient composition, *Out of Time*.

'Do you like Aveparthe's *Landscapes over the Sea*?'

'Yes, and *Outer Tehom* by that Ukrainian drone guy, Oleg Puzan', she enthused, pouring some German beers and stepping out onto the balcony. 'Be careful, it's not very safe', she said as his facial expression changed with the creak of metal wires. The storm had passed, and now silence reigned in the courtyard below.

'Thank you', he said.

'For what?'

'Helping me.'

'You are a guest in my country, it was my duty.'

'Duty?'

'Pleasure', she corrected herself.

For a while he stood at the bookshelves, glass in hand, head to one side, reading esoteric titles by Mircea Eliade, Titus Burckhardt, and Aleksander Zinovyev. He felt a pang of jealousy that she owned a signed copy of Dmitry Merezhkovsky's *Death of the Gods*, and *Against Liberalism*, a collection of essays assembled by Dugin in consultation with Alain de Benoist. His fingers settled on a large, familiar volume. 'I see you like Tolkien?' he said.

'There was a time when owning *The Lord of the Rings* was a revolutionary act', reminisced Ekaterina. Like Heidegger, Tolkien was concerned with the rise of the machine, the massification of everything. Are you familiar with Dugin's book *Martin Heidegger: The Philosophy of Another Beginning*?'

'That was published by the Radix people, right?'

'Yes, a beautiful edition. I have an English-language version in my bedroom.' Tom followed her, accepting the copy as she took it from the bedside table.

She explained that her participation in the Right was inspired by Mikhail Antonov and Sergei Kurginyan's economic vision for a new Russia. 'I also have ecological concerns', she explained. 'For me, the preservation of Russia's natural habitat is a primary objective. I hate the fact that the forests have been logged, lakes poisoned, and the Aral is now a dust bowl. I love traditional buildings. I want to fight the *malyi narod* agenda, like crime, alcoholism, dissolution of family values, and the lack of idealism amongst young people.'

'Noble intentions.'

'I am an idealist in a land of pessimists!'

'And a mystic', he added, pointing to a book on Sufism.

'I have many interests and many appetites!' She wandered into the kitchen, pulling open the fridge. 'You want another drink?' He answered in the affirmative and she fired the cork from a bottle of sparkling wine, the contents frothing madly, spurting everywhere. After a glass or so,

Ekaterina dipped her fingers into a bowl of honey and reached out provocatively for his mouth. 'You have sweet tooth?' He gripped her wrist and licked her thumb. She bent into him, tonguing his ear, golden fingers wrenching his shirt while he opened her blouse, clutching at the brassiere's metal catch, unzipping trousers, sending them sliding to reveal crimson knickers.

They fell into bed and made love to the rhythm of rain tip-tapping on windowpanes. He could feel Ekaterina's hips suck him deep inside and hear hot words of encouragement to push harder. She was lying beneath him when she came to orgasm, eyes closed, hands gripping his shoulders. His mouth was on her throat, panties coiled around a leather belt, black shoes pointing north and west.

Afterwards they lay together, listening to water pipes gurgle.

'Tell me more about England', she said.

'What do you want to know?'

'Do you all live in cottages with thatched rooves?'

'Of course!'

'And roses, are there always roses in your gardens?'

'Naturally. And we stop everything for tea with jam and scones at three o'clock.'

'Really?'

'You look surprised. I thought you had studied English culture.'

'You must not mock me', Ekaterina smiled. 'We were told you were a very polite people. That you would wait in line for a red bus and let ladies sit first.'

'Only in the suburbs', he replied. 'In the city it is dog eat dog.'

'What is suburbs?'

'I'll explain later', he promised. They disentangled their bodies, wrapping themselves in crumpled sheets, padding barefoot into the lounge to take coffee. Ekaterina watched him over the rim of a big cup. Tom leaned forward and touched her flushed cheek.

'You were wonderful', he said.

'Are you sure?' His hand was still resting against her blushing face. She did not withdraw, but did not melt with emotion either. There was a challenge in her tone now. 'You mean it?'

'Yes, I mean it', he confessed, as much to himself as to her. Outside, the rain had stopped, and stars shone like embossed rhinestones on black suede. 'A lovely night', he said. She put down her steaming drink and embraced him. Her warm tongue probed deep. Then with a wicked smile, she slipped his right hand between her legs and nodded towards the bedroom, 'Again', she said, 'I like strong man in lovemaking.'

Tom lay where he fell, bedcovers pushed back, completely naked. The curtains were half drawn, and there, opposite his half-open eyes, beside the window pane, body bleached by the pale white moon, Ekaterina sat cross-legged, staring at him like a manifestation of Priya, the Slavonic goddess of love and spring. A towel hung over her shoulder. Motionless, she gazed at him from under long lashes, mouth pouting, her expression serious.

'Come to bed or you will catch cold.' The caring tone in his voice frightened him.

'Do you mean to stay long?' She spoke softly, like someone scared of being overheard.

'We'll talk in the morning', he replied. 'Let's sleep now.' The moonlight cast a cold glow over her right cheek, her mouth hung open, a soundless sigh perched on puckering lips. Tom closed his eyelids tightly and tried to sleep. He heard a metallic noise and felt Ekaterina's weight press down on the mattress. She was sitting beside him, arms outstretched across the pillows. Tom coughed. She leaned into him, nudging his neck with her forehead. They kissed. Tom held onto her for a long time, asking himself if it was possible to feel so strongly so quickly for another person? Any normal male feelings of mere sexual gratification, conquest, and the urge for a quick exit strategy seemed to have vanished. 'Are you afraid of what is happening?' he eventually asked.

She did not reply. Ekaterina had drawn back, propping herself against the head of the bed. The towel rose and fell with her breathing. She watched him with quiet interest, something like how he imagined a scientist might study a laboratory rat. Then she took his hand. Her fingers played chase across cotton.

'No, I am angry.'

'Angry?'

'How we Russians have let things come to this.' Her frail voice was distant and low-pitched.

'How we Europeans, you mean?'

When he was sure she had fallen asleep, he got up and stood at the window, looking out over bridges and domes glowing under a corona of red light. A gull rose on an updraft of air, wings gliding against the sun, sailing far on the estuary's wind. He longed to feel the freedom of the breeze carrying him in its ebb and flow, to know that whichever way it took him, he could find his way home.

Over his shoulder, Tom could hear the rise and fall of her chest, sucking and blowing sounds through linen.

'I'm going to have to leave', he whispered to himself. 'Leave this place.' Then, looking down at Ekaterina, 'Leave you.'

$$***$$

At that very moment, Peter Janssen received clearance from his commanders in the European underground to proceed with Operation Hydra. He had been fully briefed by his Spetsnaz counterpart on logistics and tactics during the journey back from Pulkovo airport, after dropping Ulrick Hoffman off for his flight to Frankfurt. Janssen's commander, a man called Geir, headquartered in Norway, told him, 'The assassination would be the starting pistol, just like the shooting of Archduke Ferdinand in Sarajevo.'

- ❖ 'Our accommodation of President Babel's desire to re-populate Russia exemplifies our Eastern alignment with the Islamic world', says Joshua Meyer, Tel Aviv's representative to Central and Eastern Europe;
- ❖ 'Our vision for Europe and Russia is a multi-ethnic, multi-tiered, and multi-layered commonwealth of partners and associates stretching from the Atlantic Ocean to the Caspian Sea. We will expand this empire of opportunity, transforming the various communities we reach', says Nicolas Sarkozy, independent political consultant to the EU;
- ❖ In an interview widely circulated among the nationalist underground across Europe and Russia, Alexander Dugin speaks once again of 'sacred geography' and the battle for Hyperborea. 'As I said in my article "The Hand is Stretching for the Holster", this will be decided by war. The father of all things';
- ❖ Russian nationalist guerrilla units bomb pipelines running across the Caspian Sea's southern rim.

6.

Moscow has only just woken up, and Russians have only just started to recognise their identity. With every day, Russian nationalists are gaining more and more support across the country.—Alexander Belov

Four hundred marchers came down Ulitsa Marata, chanting 'Russkiy! Russkiy! *Russia for Russians!*' The columns bore their icons aloft, crowds coming together in the shade of unfurled gonfalons. Their opponents smashed shop windows and raided the Atrium shopping mall. The *Bozhaya Volya*, or God's Will Movement, began fighting pitched battles with scattered groups of Leftists hiding behind their black balaclavas, each side beating the other down the whole length of Liteyny Prospekt. Two Blacks with White girlfriends were cornered by the Nekrasov Museum. '*Blyat!*' the patriots were screaming, dragging them to the nearest bridge and throwing them off into the water below.

Alyosha and Alexei were in the forefront, standing under a banner with an orange snake clenched in a fist, giving orders and directing the action as they charged the Bloc's lines. Nikita, wearing a black shirt in honour of the Hundred, was in the vanguard, leading students in linking arms and singing with Pamyat flags:

Slav'sya, Slav'sya rodina-rossiya!
Skoz'veka I grozyty proshla!
I siyayet solntse nad toboyu
I sud'ba tvoya svetla!

Above the ancient Moscow Kremlin
waves the banner with the two-headed eagle

and the sacred words resound:
Be glorious, Russia – my Motherland!

Vehicles were torched on Nevsky. Both sides faced off
against the police, who met them in full riot gear, firing
Tac 700 Pepperball launchers and chloroance tophenone
gas into their massed ranks. Armed officers grabbed protesters in armlocks as they fled down Ulitsa Chaykovsogo.
'We had tried to reason with both groups', a spokesman
for the police said later, when he was being interviewed
on Channel 5. 'But there was no sense to it, just chaos everywhere. We have a duty to the public to maintain law
and order and that is what we did!' Sporadic skirmishes
continued in Zakharyevskaya and Tavricheskaya. Nikita
was arrested on the Naberezhnaya Robespyea, trying to
flee after the nationalists had successfully stormed the
Left's podium outside the university. Nikki's head was
pushed between spread knees, his hands cuffed from behind.

'We are all Limonov now!' he kept shouting as police
surrounded the students in Tavrichsky Sad. In Ploschad
Iskussy, Alyosha was using homemade Molotov cocktails
against a police cordon. The FSB had forced VKontakte to
shut down their social network. Rubber bullets whizzed.
When the dogs were loosed, everyone scattered, clambering to escape. German Shepherds dragged pony-tailed
girls to the ground, and boys beat the animals back with
anything that came to hand.

At 3 that afternoon Grigori, accompanied by the Rector
Valentine Bondarenko, Dimitri, Alexander, and Svetlana
gave a press conference on the university steps.

'Although we do not condone the violence, today's
events were completely predictable. Extreme Leftist fac-
tions, given succour by anti-Russian elements, have been
assaulting and harassing both ourselves and our international guests from the start of this event. Many of our
young people are being told lies about their country's past,
the reasons for its current political malaise, and the op-

tions for a better future. What occurred today was a short, sharp punch in the solar plexus of our globalist masters. Let me remind you of Dmitry Dyomushkin of the Russian's Movement's prophetic words: "Speaking about the extinction of the Russians . . . There will be no changes for the better for you if you cannot grasp this. No chance for you, or for your children.'"

As his voice trailed off from the agreed script, the questions came flying. 'Do you support fascism? Do you condone Anders Breivik? Do you deny the Holocaust?' A look of indignant contempt sailed like a gunboat across Grigori's face.

'Your questions tell me all I need to know about the spin your paymasters intend to take on today's disturbances, as well as on the issues that confront us now and will challenge us in the future. Your adherence to an invented past will trap us into reliving our tragedies time and time again.' And with that, the delegation withdrew behind the university's gates. The verbal altercation was rapidly edited and transmitted to the whole country through the controlled media.

Meanwhile, President Babel and his bodyguards had been ambushed in their armoured Chevrolet. The traffic lights on the Neva embankment had been rigged to flick to red as he moved off the bridge. Suddenly, three men opened fire with small arms, using armour-piercing bullets made from depleted uranium to riddle the convoy. Two others stepped from behind sphinx statues, aiming grenade launchers, and then there was flaring phosphorus burning everyone to death. Rumour had it that foreign security forces were responsible. Others said that Babel's people had fallen out with the Yellow Mafia. Within hours, a bloody feud between the rival oligarchs and leading *biznesmeny* from the brewing, banking, printing, and electronics syndicates had led to multiple murders by sniper fire, poison, or a sharp blade between the ribs.

❖ The Duma holds an emergency meeting ratifying
  Prime Minister Viktor Akulov as Acting President;
❖ President Akulov immediately confirms Russia's
  civil government's continued intention to give succour to the Great Migration, quoting Sweden's Interior Minister Gecht in a TV debate on SVT
  World, 'Russia will only fulfil its geographic ambi-
  tion if it can accommodate people of Asiatic origin';
❖ Commentators in the World News Media start
  warning of the rise of Russian neo-Nazism, com-
  paring Russia to Germany in the 1920s;
❖ Under the auspices of an emergency act sponsored
  by George Soros at the UN, the World Bank secures
  Russia's re-entry into the G8 and begins to formu-
  late the Levantine Accords to facilitate loans to re-
  structure the Russian economy;
❖ The pro-liberal Radio Meduza, operating out of Riga, quadruples its programme output in support of
  Acting President Akulov, welcoming his efforts in
  following his predecessor's policy of guiding Russia
  back into the family of democratic nations.

They were rushing, fleeing violence on Nevsky, making
for the sanctuary of the Alexander monastery. Ignoring
the Ka-226 helicopters and the speeding police Passats,
they barely escaped the crunch of Gaz Tigr 4X4s, which
were ploughing down rioters at the intersection of Kon-
naya and Ispolkomskaya.

Hiding in Mitropolichiy sad after they heard about the
state of emergency, Ekaterina took him by the hand,
marching him down Mirgorodskaya Ulitsa, then back
along Telezhnaya in a wide arc to avoid the police cordons
of KamAZ trucks and checkpoints manned by scarf-faced
militia armed with Viyaz-SN machine pistols.

'Here in Tikhvin are graves of many great people.' Ekaterina's eyes clouded with admiration. 'Tchaikovsky, Mussorgsky, and Rimsky-Korsakov.' Then, raising her hand,
'Over there is resting place of Dostoevsky.' He turned to

follow her long finger, an iron gateway guarding the remains of the author of *Crime and Punishment*. 'Some
charnel house, no?'

They joined the back of a queue shuffling slowly towards the entrance. The old, sick, and lonely hobbled
staccato-style up the steps. Ekaterina asked, 'Are you sure
you want to go?'

Tom nodded, the great Cathedral doors opening, swallowing them like Jonah's whale. Inside, they were lost in
deep darkness, broken only occasionally by the shimmer
of tallow candles sending a warm ripple across icons. The
recitation of liturgy was accompanied by the swish of dark
robes brushing stone, solemn priests circling under the
dome.

He was conscious of people perpetually crossing themselves and considered following suit, but his instinctive
secularism still held strong. Tom estimated there must
have been two hundred people there. Old babushkas
wrapped in shawls, bowing fervently, prostrated themselves before painted saints, gilded frames, pock-marked
prophets, and apostles rising in a pantheon of flickering
candlelight.

Then, emerging out of the scented fog, a procession of
bearded priests came walking towards the chancel. From
the gallery above, a choir filled dead air with a song so
heart-rending you could feel the isolation of a Siberian
winter. Ekaterina stood still, staring straight ahead. Tom
shifted uncomfortably from left to right. His atheist incli-
nations were completely overwhelmed by this ritual assault on all five senses. It was hard to imagine how the
Marxists could have suppressed such outpourings of faith
for so many years. Only 10 percent of the Christian
churches had survived the famine years of the 1920s, when
the Party seized altar gold and silver plates to melt down
for bullion. Synagogues were untouched. Then there was
the Kamchatka martyrdom of thousands upon thousands
of the faithful. In the handful of enclaves that held out,
the authorities broke up prayer meetings with squads of

secret police wielding steel batons and sledgehammers.

It seemed incredible that Lenin and his disciples could have upstaged Jesus. But, perhaps they had not. Maybe, they had only temporarily substituted for him in a failed attempt to pervert the Russian soul. The congregation responded in unison throughout the service. They queued to buy candles, kneeling and kissing icons. The Professor found the atmosphere positively medieval. Commanding huge respect, crones with wrinkled leather skin and curling yellow fingernails who were bent double moved between the flowing shawls of Byzantine priests. Ancient matriarchs performed some special rite known to them alone, people bowing as they passed and making room for them wherever they decided to rest their legs. At the high point of the service, the triple blessing, they assumed to lead the congregation, stumbling onto their knees, shuffling on their bellies across the stone floor, foreheads lowered to the ground as the liturgy soared to its peak.

'Where were you baptised?' she asked as they moved in step.

'I don't know.'

'Heathen!' she said in so low a register that no one could hear. 'You call yourself civilised?' He felt her fingernails dig into his palm.

'Are you offering me salvation?'

Her voice came back in a whisper. 'You are beyond redemption, you'd best ask the blessing of the Great Patriarch himself!'

Standing in line, he looked on as Ekaterina kissed the hand of the priest before receiving communion. Then it was his turn, and he hesitantly stepped forward. His partner glanced back with a look of encouragement. 'Time to make good', she said. Tom felt frail fingertips brush his forehead as he bowed before the chalice and spoon. Looking up, four-square into the blind gaze of the old man before him, he saw rather than heard the words form on cracked lips. Syllables birthed from asthmatic lungs. Straining to understand, he moved aside, his palate burn-

ing with the after-taste of vinegar, the wraith-like sensa-
tion of this man's Hebrew God caressing him with a ca-
daverous hand. The whole experience left him feeling as if
a shard of glass was moving in his conscience.

Walking back through the nave, only the old remained,
clattering on sticks, sheltering in echoes. He asked if they
had nowhere else to go. 'After all, it was cold outside and
they had heard about the trouble in the streets.'

'No', she said. 'They are the *raskol'niki*. You say, "Old
Believers", remnants of another time and place.' His next
question was drowned out by the chant rising from a
priest standing in a beam of light, black robes and runic
markings shining, head thrown back, singing a hymn to
an Old Testament God. You could hear the desperation in
the intonation. Tom asked himself, where was this God
when the serfs starved, when Stalin imprisoned people for
the way they looked at him, or when the German panzers
swept through the cornfields? His silence was deafening
then, but he had found his voice now, now that the Wall
was cracked and the whisperers were fewer in number.

As the huge doors swung open, symbolic of the resur-
rection in Orthodox tradition, grey light burst forth,
showering down upon them, casting elongated shadows
far back into the church. White doves rose in a flurry of
flapping wings and snowy feathers. The cityscape wore a
gossamer sheen. At such moments, the Leningrad of the
1930s re-emerged, buildings taking on an ominous aspect,
dark and overwhelming like giant stone commissars
watching everything you did, listening to every word you
said, Comrade Yezhov's eyes behind every window.

An hour later, they were stopped outside the Moscow
station, at the halfway point down Nevsky. A policeman
approached as they photographed the obelisk crowned
with its golden star.

'I need to see your papers', he demanded.

'Why?' Ekaterina interceded.

'Because it is a state of emergency, and foreigners were

involved in the assassination of the President!' said a voice from over their shoulders. Turning, they saw an older man in a green raincoat. 'We are checking many people!' The Professor noted the slicked back hair and cigarette dangling from his mouth. The uniformed officer reached for him, trying to get a grip on his collar. Tom stepped back, pushing his hand away. There was a brief struggle.

'Resisting arrest, this is serious', laughed the plain-clothes man. 'We have been arresting your type all day!' He indicated for his younger colleague to stand aside. A small crowd of onlookers formed a horseshoe around them. Taxi drivers were honking horns. 'Do you have your passport?'

'No, he leaves it in a safe deposit box at the hotel!' Ekaterina sounded exasperated.

'Is this true?' The older man asked, turning to Tom.

'Yes', he said, taking her lead.

'What is your name? Where are you staying?' Tom told him and he wrote down the details in a notebook. 'And why are you here?'

'I'm attending the conference.'

'Agitator', he smirked, then looked at Ekaterina. 'Don't you have pretty young women in your own country?'

'I'm here for the conference!' There was an undertow of anger in the Englishman's tone.

'So you say, and we have all heard about the trouble caused by this conference.' He stepped up close to Tom and blew smoke directly into his face. There was a ripple of laughter from the gathering crowd. 'Foreigners with big ideas bringing trouble to our city.' Columns of people poured out of the station entrance. The interrogator's younger accomplice tapped the handle of the gun at his hip. Ekaterina typed a number into her cell phone.

'British Consul, please', she said loudly in Russian. The inquisitor threw Ekaterina a hateful look and, walking away, brushed the girl aside with a stab of his elbow. His sidekick spat in Tom's face before following his boss into the fast-moving traffic on the Ligovsky Prospekt.

Tom glared after them. Ekaterina wiped his face with a handkerchief, kissing his cheek. 'You look worried', she said. 'Don't be scared, it's going to happen.'

'But those things he said—'

'What things?'

'About you!'

'You already must know people think those things? Young Russian girl with a foreign man, it is in all the hotels and bars.'

'I don't think about us like that!'

'Then don't.'

They wandered down Nevsky, checking behind them to make sure they were not being followed. A large group of Nashi youth were gathered under red and white banners at the gaping black mouth of the Mayakovskaya metro station. A clean-cut commissar was regaling the crowd outside the Nevsky Forum hotel through a megaphone. 'Our famous patriots, the United Russia party?' Ekaterina cursed. 'Shit for brains!'

'What's he saying?'

'No Western interference in Russian affairs . . . the honour of our people . . . '

'Sounds ominous!'

'Sounds vacuous!'

'You are not impressed?'

'Not really. You do not need to be clairvoyant. Nashi, or *Ours*, are really *Theirs*. They are the antithesis of the old Ukrainian Pora, the Serbian Otpor, and Georgia's Kmara movements. The original Nashi leader, Vasily Yakemenko, took $500,000 to re-invent Komsomol. What we need is another Narodnaya Volya or Mladorossitsi movement! There are groups called "the Shield" working in Moscow. They raid illegal's barracks and work with the police to combat the Uzbeks.'

'You don't rate Putin's legacy?'

'Putin was a doorman for the oligarchs. His success rested on improving the lifestyles of the mafia. That's why when the police clear the streets of our people, these charlatans are allowed to speak. Russian democracy is paper-thin.'

'But . . .'

She shut him down. 'No ifs or buts. We need people like Oleg Kasin and the Russian National Unity, Rodina and A Just Russia. Read Andrei Saveliev's *Political Mythology* or his *The Image of the Enemy*, then all will be clear to you. Personally, I refuse to be a consumer, blindly following fashions and the global trends determined by one-worldists who manage our media for their own purposes!'

'Look', he said, 'I wanted to hit that policeman!'

'That is exactly what they hoped for, an excuse to get you alone in their car, take your wallet, everything!'

'What made you think of calling the Consul?'

'The cats hunt the mice, and the dogs chase the cats.'

'Some things never change.' They turned onto Malaya Morskaya. Passing number 17, Ekaterina's eyes widened, pointing up to an apartment that looked down on the street through large, clear windows.

'That is where Gogol wrote his satire, *The Government Inspector.*'

'True irony.'

'*Plus ca change, plus c'est la meme chose.*'

7.

The cult of money-making of the consumer society, proliferation and legalisation of sexual and social vice, protection of the interests of parasitic minorities at the expense of the majority, the limitation of liberties of the creative majority, 'cyborgisation' of people, extreme individualism, egoism, birth rates fall, destruction of the cult of family and religion, profanation of traditional values.—Anonymous, Hook Sprava, 2008

They reached her grandfather's place, a block typical of its period: three storeys high, topped with pigeon-grey metal. A stone balustrade ran the length of the first floor. Balconies were balanced with trepidation, supported on varicose-veined pillars, projecting out like Neanderthals' foreheads.

Ekaterina punched a worn button on a rusted intercom buried in the wall. 'We'll be safe here', she was saying. There was a buzz and crackle. Then she pushed the door open onto a big black belly full of foul air. The lift was out of order, twisted wire sealing the shaft. Stone stairwells were filled with the whimpering of scolded children.

A door slammed above. The weighty smell of yesterday's potatoes swept down the hallway. This had once been a fashionable part of the city. Now, for so many of its tenants, the bitter years since Gorbachev's *glasnost* had blown away the old certainties. The familiar communal routine of bygone years was a fond memory for the older generation, but complete bullshit to the young. Spray-paint and dog excrement smeared landings. Ekaterina led him through flickering lights, electric wiring hanging loose like cat entrails. The sparks tangoing on the ceiling were reflected in the putrid pools at their feet as they moved like a modern-day Theseus and Ariadne ever deeper into the Minotaur's lair.

Eventually, halting in front of a dented door, she knocked hard twice. Then waited, rapping twice again, in some pre-arranged code. A moment later, Tom heard the grating grind of bolts being thrown and the rattle of a chain. Backlit by a naked bulb, a small, thin man came stooping over the doorstep. She hugged him tightly, speaking in familiar Russian. Then, gesturing to Tom, they were formally introduced. 'Herman', he said, handshakes exchanged before the Englishman stepped over the threshold.

Inquisitorial eyes set in rheumy crinkles scanned the Professor surreptitiously. Herman's protective instincts caused him to check out the man his grand-daughter had brought to him.

'You were caught in the troubles?' he asked.

'Only a little', she said soothingly. 'We got off Nevsky in time.' Herman pointed towards the television with an arthritic finger.

'Rossia One coverage has been interesting.'

- ❖ International news media report that the Russian Army is mounting a coup;
- ❖ A spokesman for the Utro Rossii movement is quoted as saying, 'We are working with the armed forces in order to stabilise the situation after President Babel's death';
- ❖ Konstantin Poltoranin, former spokesman for the Federal Migratory Service, dismissed for stating 'the survival of the White race is at stake', is reinstated and his views become federal policy;
- ❖ Members of the 45th Special Reconnaissance Regiment storm Building 14 in Moscow's Kremlin, where the new President, Viktor Akulov, was holding an emergency meeting to discuss the crisis with high-profile representatives from Brussels, New York, and Tel Aviv;

❖ Later, the attendees at the meeting are shown being frog-marched out into Ivanovskaya Square,
   where Tos-1A MRL missile launchers are seen aiming at the ionic columned neo-classical façade.

'I see events are moving in our favour', Tom said smug-
ly.

'Don't be too sure', Herman advised. 'I saw how the last
coup d'etat under Aleksandr Rutskoy ended after Yeltsin
awarded himself Extraordinary Executive Powers. Tanks
from the Taman Division shelled Moscow's White House,
the mayoral office closed, and the Ostankino TV centre
was stormed. Tens of thousands of Russians took to the
streets of Moscow, including members of the National
Salvation Front and militants of Russian National Unity.
But when General Grachev went over to Yeltsin, it was all
over for the short-lived Rutskoy-Khasbulatov regime and
all those who tried to preserve the Supreme Soviet and the
Constitution. The White House was assaulted by Vympel
and Alpha units. Within hours, Yeltsin declared "the fa-
scistic-Communist armed rebellion in Moscow shall be
suppressed within the shortest period". Afterwards, legis-
lation was enacted by presidential decree, applying heavy
sanctions against fascism, chauvinism, and racial hatred.
The rise of Vladimir Zhirinovsky's ultra-nationalist Liberal
Democratic Party scared Yeltsin, though. Newspapers like
Den, *Sovietskaya Rosiya*, and *Pravda* were banned.'
   Inside Herman's apartment, the rooms were cold. It
seemed the heating was constantly failing. 'It's freezing,
Pappa!' Ekaterina admonished him, fussing around the
place. He waved her concerns away with a 'Ba, soon I'll be
dead anyway', type of reply. Then, turning to Tom, she
said, 'It loses energy through bad windows.' From what
the newcomer could see, the flat comprised two bedrooms
and a lounge with a good, high ceiling and a chair placed
so as to give a view back over the road they had just
crossed. Tom realised her grandfather had probably been
watching them walk hand-in-hand from the underground

station. The bathroom was small and the kitchen even smaller. A St Andrew's cross hung on the wall. Heavy curtains had been selected not so much for their aesthetic quality as their capacity to insulate. Nineteenth-century furniture was crammed full of books by Schwartz-Bostunich and Nilus. There were texts of all descriptions: technical, political, and historical. Tom read the spines of novels like Bryusov's *Pale Horse*, Rozanov's *Apocalypse of Our Time*, Solovyov's *A Story of the Anti-Christ*, and Andrei Bely's *Vision of the Coming Kingdom of the Beast*. There was a chess set on a coffee table.

'My ancestors are part German', her grandfather said in halting English. Then, noticing where Tom's eyes had settled, he continued in Russian, with Ekaterina translating. 'You admire the game?'

'I play a little', Tom replied.

'Kasparov is a genius, but he should have stayed out of politics.'

'And Karpov?'

'A KGB mechanist.' In that moment they understood each other. There was mutual recognition of kindred spirits across continents and generations.

'Chess is not everything, but it is nearly everything', he speculated. 'I can remember when I came here with my first wife, Sveta, in 1956. It was just after Khrushchev had denounced Comrade Stalin at the Twentieth Party Congress. "Comrades", he said, "we must abolish the cult of the individual decisively, once and for all".' The old man's eyes meandered for a moment. 'We never achieved that!'

'Putin followed in that tradition.'

The old man's eyes flared. 'Different tradition', he wheezed. 'It is true we have always had strong autocrats, but this did not start with the Bolsheviks. First there was five centuries of Tsarist absolutism, beginning from the time we drove the Mongol hordes from our land. Then there were people like Metropolitan Macarius and Iury Krizhanich, author of *Politika*, who believed in enlightened absolutism. Krizhanich died fighting with the Polish army defending Vienna from the Turks. Patriarch Nikon, Khomiakov, Feofan Prokopovich, and Tatishchev were also conservative Orthodox patriots of the *pravoslavnyi* variety. The Church was moving back then towards a national self-consciousness, *nationalnoe samosoznanie*. Even Pushkin himself regarded "inequality as a law of nature".' Herman draped an arm around Ekaterina to steady himself. 'Then there was Shcherbatov, Speransky, and Karamzin. They were followed by Chaadaev, Gogol, and the Slavophile school.'

'Very many thinkers!'

'And many more, too! After 1855 there were Katkov, Samarin, Aksakov, Leontiev and Witte. Later, Kavelin, Chicherin, Gradovsky, Soloviev, Nesterov, Sergei Bulgakov, the Szemstvo movement, Struve, Shipov, and of course Stolypin, assassinated by Dimitri Bogrov at the Kiev Opera before he could save the Imperial dynasty.'

'And Bogrov's real name was Mordekhai Gershkovich, a Jewish provocateur.'

'Yes!'

'But anyway, I'm sure you would agree with me that the Paschal Edict was the beginning of the end. It killed the notion of the apostolic role of the Tsar. That perception was only partially corrected by the symbolic canonisation of the patriotic Patriarch Germogen in 1913.'

'And four years later?'

'The Revolution, of course.'

'Another *coup d'etat!*' he was corrected quickly. 'My . . .' Then, looking over at Ekaterina, he corrected himself, 'Our favourite author Solzhenitsyn said, "You must understand the leading Bolsheviks who took over Russia were not Russians. They hated Russians. Driven by ethnic hatred, they tortured and slaughtered millions of Russians without a shred of remorse . . . It cannot be overstated. Bolshevism committed the greatest human slaughter of all time. The fact that the world is ignorant of or uncaring about this enormous crime is proof that the global media is in the hands of the perpetrators".'

'Yes, even Israeli journalists now admit that 40 percent of the top-ranking officials in the Soviet system were Jewish Chekists. Gengrihky Yagoda alone was responsible for the deaths of at least 10 million Christian Russians.'

'The percentage is much higher, my friend. Zionism and Marxism are brothers.' Herman sighed. 'And they still operate the same way. Your Robert Wilton, a British journalist for *The London Times* was here at the time of the Revolution. He said, "Bolshevism is not Russian. It's essentially non-national. Its leaders belong almost entirely to the race that lost its country and its nationhood long ago. In April 1918, the Russian government, including 384 peoples' commissars, was represented by 2 negroes, 13 Russians, 15 Chinamen, 22 Armenians and Georgians, and more than 300 Jews. Of the last, 264 had come to Russia from the United States during the Revolution . . . The revolutionary pseudo-Jews thus destroying Russia's hopes of national revival and dragging the country into chaos".'

'I am familiar with his works *Russia's Agony* and *The Last Days of the Romanovs.*'

'Did you know his writing was censored? He named names, identified aliens operating under assumed Russian and Polish identities. After that, he was threatened with murder.'

'I can well imagine, they operate like a mafia.'

'They run the American and the Russian mafia. Who talks of the Ukrainian Holodmor? What did the former Sephardic Rabbi of Jerusalem, Ovadia Yosef, say about Palestinians at his Passover speech? "It is forbidden to be merciful to them, you must send missiles to annihilate them . . . the Lord shall return the Arabs' deeds on their own heads, waste their seed, and exterminate them, devastate them, and vanish them from this world".'

'So much for their *never again* protestations about the Holocaust!'

'Comrade Lenin was financed by the Warburgs, the plutocrat Jacob Henry Schiff, and the Khun, Loeb & Company banking house. The first Politburo was, like the Cheka, overwhelmingly foreign. Your own Winston Churchill said, "There is no need to exaggerate the part played in the creation of Bolshevism by the international and for the most part atheistical Jews. It is certainly a very great one." Just read what Hugo Koehler of the US intelligence mission said when reporting back to Washington about our *gibel rossii,* our supposed Civil War.' Herman's eyes flashed. 'They say truth is stranger than fiction. I once read a novel called *Biarritz . . .*'

Then, thinking he was talking too much politics, he tried to change the subject. 'These districts', he gestured out of the window, 'were *mikroraioni,* little towns of their own, with their own shops and schools, and more and more people came and lived there. Hardly anyone had homes in the centre of town anymore.'

'Indeed', Tom said, picking up the old man's thread, trying to place the conversation back on a literary track. 'I think Berdayev spoke of Dostoevksy's gestalt, something about faith requiring space unfettered by form, as being real Christianity.' The old man, reassured that he was not being too outspoken, was not to be outdone.

'"And now we stare into the abyss of modernity; constrained, no space for our inner soul. We still at least have a Russian soul. We see through the artificial plastic personalities so common in the West." Dostoevsky was a *pochvenniki,* a radical native-soil conservative. In his *Diary of a Writer,* he talks of the unique *natsionalnost* of every people.' There was a nod of acknowledgement on both sides before Herman continued his tale. 'Dostoevsky recognised the enemy. He told the truth. "Jews are draining the soil of Russia", he said, and he was right.' Herman shook his wise head. 'You see, he saw the *graznye,* the moneymakers, characters like Isay Fomitch Bumstein in *The House of the Dead,* for what they were. He put good counsel into the mouth of Shatov as he spoke to Stavrogin in *The Devils*: "Reduce God to the attribute of nationality? . . . on the contrary, I elevate the nation to God . . . The people is the body of God . . . The sole God bearing nation is the Russian nation".' Herman wiped away his wrinkles with the palm of a hand.

'And speaking of today, do you see the same Zionist conspiracy?'

'Well, you decide for yourself. It never ended. This war is eternal. Do you think such powerful positions in the current regime could be limited to a specific gene pool by mere chance? The Metropolitan of St Petersburg, Ioann Synchev, got their measure. Did you know that over 90 percent of Béla Kun's dictatorship in Hungary were followers of the Talmud?'

'Yes, I think David Irving wrote a book called *Uprising* which highlighted the fact that the same people were instrumental in the debacle of 1956.'

'That was not an isolated case. Khrushchev said, "That very same year, the government has found in some departments a heavy concentration of Jewish people, upwards of fifty percent of the staff". If you look further back, the Jews in interwar Romania were only 4 percent of the population, but controlled the export, transportation, insurance, textile, chemical, housing, and publishing industries. They also dominated law, medicine, journalism, and banking. The same people in Lithuania accounted for 75 percent of commercial activity. In Hungary, Jews represented over 30 percent of actors and musicians, 50 percent of attorneys, and 60 percent of the medical profession. We should be so grateful for their talents, don't you think?'

'And once they got out of the Pale of Settlement in Russia, they ran the black market in vodka and prostitution.'

'And through the Black Sea port of Odessa, dominated the trade of white flesh to the east.'

'I liked Konstantin Pobedonostev's solution to the Jewish problem: by having one-third of them killed, one-third of them converted to Christianity, and one-third driven out of the country forever.'

'If only. The Ginzburgs and Poliakovs diversified from vodka distilleries to railroads and made fortunes. Again,

Dostoevsky predicted such things in *The Adolescent*, where he turned Stendhal's *The Red and the Black* on its head, making the foolish Dolgoruky worship money and Count de Rothschilds as opposed to Napoleon. Solzhenitsyn's *Two Hundred Years Together* followed a similar theme, and despite his obvious popularity as a novelist, it remains unpublished in English.' Ekaterina poured tea she had prepared from a warm pot. Then Herman started again where he had left off.

'I know these people's tactics. Vladimir Purishkevich said, "They have an irreconcilable hatred of Russia and everything Russian", and he was right. You see, I lived under their iron heel for too long, not to see behind the lies and deception. Like Dostoevsky wrote, "A long peace always breeds cruelty, cowardice, and crude, flabby egoism, and principally mental stagnation. During a long peace, only the exploiters of people grow fat." Look how many of today's oligarchs are from that sect. Even Yuri Kanner of the Russian Jewish Congress admits this. Who were Yeltsin's post-perestroika string-pullers in the loans for shares scheme? Abramovich, Aven, Berezovsky, Friedman, Gusinsky and Khodorkovsky.'

'Men who poured millions into Yeltsin's re-election campaign.'

'Men who ran ticket-scalping scams, Avva pyramid schemes, and drove the Menatap Bank's records off a bridge into the Dybna River', Herman added. 'You know, I was one of the people to work with Vailyev on the public letter from Pamyat to Boris Yeltsin . . . "Your Jewish entourage . . . have already made good use of you and don't need you anymore. You will share the destiny of Napoleon and Hitler, etc., who were Zionist-maintained dictators . . . The aim of international Zionism is to seize power worldwide. For this reason Zionists struggle against national and religious traditions of other nations, and for this purpose they devised the Freemasonic concept of cosmopolitanism".'

'Like you, I sympathise with Vladimir Miloserdov and

former General Igor Rodionov, who demanded that the oligarchs "must return what they have looted in Russia and publicly repent to the Russian people for the crimes that Jewish terrorists and extremists have committed".'

'I am a historian of the Michael the Archangel Russian People's Union. Before that, in the 1970s, I was active in the Vityaz, you say Knight Movement, with people like the artist Ilya Glazunov, the historian Malyshev, and Lebedev, a colonel in the MVD. We formed the National Patriotic Front in 1987.'

'Is that the one Aleksander Barkashov's people split from in 1990?'

'Yes, that is so.'

'And there was Valeriy Yemelyanov, who wrote the book *Dezionisation*. He was a neo-pagan, right?'

'A mystic. *Pamyat* translates as 'Memory' in English, I think.' Herman went on, undeterred. 'Until recently, Germany was our chief trading partner, and the EU was the market for over 50 percent of our exports. Yet, so-called Westerners like Bernard-Henri Lévy, A André Glucksmann, and Alain Finkielkraut oppose our economic independence. In the centuries before these parasites began to feed off us, Russia controlled 8,660,000 square miles of land, the largest land empire in all of history, growing at a rate of 50 square miles per year for 400 years.'

'Indeed, the conquest of Kokand, Bokhara, and Khiva brought the whole of Central Asia under Tsarist rule.'

'But today, it is like we live in a science fiction story, Zamyatin's *We!*'

8.

Rossiia Est Sviataia Rus.—John Vostorgov

Tom stepped up to the podium, warm applause greeting him as he bent into the spotlight, reaching to adjust the microphone.

'Good afternoon', he began. 'It is generally acknowledged by mainstream anthropologists, linguists, and archaeologists that our common ancestors spoke a Proto-Indo-European dialect some 6,000 years ago, in the very heart of Eurasia. Liberal and Left-leaning academics, particularly in Western universities, may choose to ignore this inconvenient fact, but they can no longer flat-out deny the efficacy of such an assertion or the extensive fieldwork carried out by Vyachislav Ivanov into root languages, and Gennadii Zdanovich's archaeologists at Arkaim. Works by David Anthony and K Jones-Bley have led many great thinkers to the conclusion that the Sintashta-Petrovka culture, of which the Mandala City of Arkaim is the best preserved example, is in fact the ancient, 4,000-year-old capital of the founders of our so-called Western civilisation, those very Caucasoids who invaded Northern India, rode across the Gobi to trade with the Khans, and buried their flame-haired mummies in Urumchi. Our women were tattooed with the crescent moon of the goddess and our men with the sun representing the male god. I challenge anyone to look into the eyes of the beauty of Loulan, a woman born into the Tocharian culture of the Tarim basin nearly 4,000 years ago, and find a trace of Mongoloid blood.

'She, like her Solutrean kin on the Atlantic rim, those adventurers who moved across the ice bridge to America, would eventually see their small, fragile settlements exterminated by second peoples, the Han, Goturks, and Uy-

ghur tribes of northwest China's Bogda and Tian Shan
mountains in the first case, and the Yupik aboriginals of
Beringia coming down from the Bering Straits in the latter
instance. Could this very habitation at Arkaim be the one
referred to in the *Avesta* and the *Vedas*?'

The audience was rapt. 'Indeed, the scientific community, resistant to anything that challenged the liberal narrative, were at first unwilling to admit that this sophisti-
cated people was living parallel with the Levantines of
Egypt and Babylon. Arkaim, older than Troy and Rome,
was equipped with a storm sewage system, timber structures imbued with fire-resistant resins, and heating and
cooling systems for every dwelling. Archeoastronomists
even identified the lauburu planning pattern of the city as
being so precise, one arc-minute, that it was only with the
arrival of the almagest, two millennia later, that such precision was once again attained by mankind.'

Tom continued to enthral his spectators for a further
20 minutes, talking about the Yamnaya DNA from western Russia spreading into Europe 4,000 years ago and the
different strands of the human tree, before turning to the
central theme of his polemic. 'And today, we see a vast
shadow creep over Eurasia once again. A pestilence which
threatens to tip the geopolitical tectonic plates as the East
moves West.' He took a sip of water. 'And from where
does this shadow arise? It emanates from those who jeal-
ously guard their monopolies over your labour and resent
your new-found freedom after centuries of servitude. But
already, this transformation in fortune, this hemispheric
shift of the last few days, offers us new possibilities for renewal and rebirth. Can we, the Europid descendants of
the nomadic adventurers of which I have spoken, rise
again after the collapse?' Tom stopped to pour more water
into the tumbler resting on the lectern. 'Mainstream historians are looking increasingly aghast as the views of a
controversial genius like Anatole Klyosov begin to chime
with the material being unearthed in the most unpromis-
ing geological strata. Every day, it is becoming clearer and

clearer that the anecdotes of Ancient Greece about the Pillar Peoples are being proved correct in the vastness of the steppes . . . '

There was almost exaltation in his words. All eyes were on him. 'There is another way', he insisted. 'Our original way. *Ar-ka* means sky and *Im* means earth. Arkaim is a place where the earth reaches the sky. In Alex Sparkey's words, the East and West are fused here. Today, in Russia, we feel that mankind is faced by the necessity to choose Oneness. Western culture must come into unity with Eastern Orthodox wisdom. If this happens, the hegemony that we once took for granted in the Land of Cities will be restored.' With that flourish, he brought the house down. Grigori and Dimitry stormed the stage to congratulate him. 'You have conjured up Iliodor's vision once again!' they shouted as a standing ovation resounded in the auditorium.

Ekaterina took an urgent call in the middle of the after-conference dinner. At first, she could barely make out the words over the singing of White Army songs: 'We will march to fight for Holy Russia, and spill as one our blood for her!' When she did comprehend what had happened, she dragged Tom from the room, flagging down a taxi to her grandfather's district.

Chasing down torch beams, tripping over hose pipes in the smoke-filled air, they could hear the coarse dialects of firemen using spray to clear the bitter tang of the accelerant used to firebomb the block. Her grandfather's apartment was full of scorched plaster and charred books. Ekaterina was crying, imagining the worst from the very moment the emergency was raised.

'I can't believe it', she kept saying through the gaps between her fingers. 'What if . . . ?' Her words trailed off. They both understood. Tom's arm curled around her shoulders in an attempt to comfort her.

'There!' he said, pointing at a figure wrapped in a damp blanket emerging from the bedroom. Ekaterina looked up, her face screaming relief.

'*Dedushka, dedushka!*' she shouted, running towards the sombre survivor coming towards them out of the darkness. '*Kak de la?*' Herman took her face in his hands.

'*Orchin kraseeva devoushka*', he reassured her, '*horosho, horosho!*' Herman's eyes met Tom's over Ekaterina's shoulder. 'So history repeats itself. We have our civil war. It is time for a strong man in Russia again', he said, coughing through smoke-filled lungs. 'The question, of course, is, are men like you and Grigori strong enough?' His face beseeched the Englishman to protect his girl by whatever means necessary.

After getting Herman to hospital, they returned to the Astoria. There were four or five threatening messages on his phone. Tom recognised Arkady's voice and hit call back, screaming down the phone about avenging the fire-bombing.

'You should let us handle it!' she insisted.

'No, this is personal.'

'Are you trying to impress me or my grandfather?'

'Maybe both of you.' While Tom was shaving Ekaterina, flicked to and fro through the TV channels:

❖ Traditionalist sympathisers use the Internet monitor Roskomnadzor to prevent Navalny and Leftist activists from accessing Firechat mesh-networking social media in order to foment discord and demonstrations;

❖ Troops loyal to the new regime are busy removing liberal agitators from rallying sites in Red Square and the Moskvoretsky Bridge in Moscow;

❖ General Yegor Moskvin appears on state television. Speaking from the Kremlin, he declares that martial law will be imposed from midnight, following the barricading of roads leading to immigrant communities and the sealing off of parts of urban areas where they are the demographic majority;

- ❖ The UN, EU, and World Bank insist that Russia returns to a model of democracy acceptable to the world community;
- ❖ Nationalist composer Mussorgsky's opera *Boris Godunov* is played continuously on the radio;
- ❖ T-90 battle tanks and BTR-80 armoured personnel carriers block the Tretye Transportnoye Koltso and Garden Ring roads in Moscow;
- ❖ The Lefortovo tunnel is sealed and the M10 between the capital and St Petersburg is made into a strategic corridor, defended by air and ground forces;
- ❖ Unknown gunmen open fire on police and army units imposing order in Nizhny Tagil;
- ❖ The Pushkinsky District in St Petersburg is militarised, becoming a logistics centre to support brigades facing any potential EU threat via the Finnish border;
- ❖ GROM units conduct mass arrests of drug dealers, seizing stockpiles of weapons as well as quantities of heroin, cocaine, and synthetic marijuana known as 'spice' in Kemerov, Nalchik, Shakhy, Orsk, Balashikva, Rybinsk, and Korov.

Eventually, she came to the bathroom door, leaned on the wood frame, and looked hard at him.

'I want to be the next Sabine or Yevgenia Khasis.'

'In prison and hunted, you mean?'

'The new government will release Yevgenia from the camps.'

'But Sabine's got a harder job in France.'

'You know I am descended from the Sarmatian and Alans, the tribes that gave birth to the legends about the Amazons.' She broke off as Tom looked up from the bowl.

'And brought the myths that would eventually become King Arthur and the Holy Grail to Britain.'

'I see you have recalled your classes about Batradz', she laughed.

'And the warrior women buried in the Pokrovka mounds on the Kazakh border.'

'Then you know our girls were not allowed to wed until they had killed a man in battle.'

'They also cut off their right breasts!'

She bent forward. 'Not all the stories are true.'

'Thank God.'

'You know I am a believer in the *beregini*, the Slavic protector goddesses.'

'Not necessarily a good Orthodox girl, then?'

'*Nyet!* Below, old traditions remain.'

Tom smiled as Ekaterina walked over to the window, sliding her hand up and down the lined drapes. 'We believe the sacred feminine cocoons our lives, being conceived in the womb and returning to Mother Earth, after we die. It is a simple cycle, much less complex than the Holy Trinity of Father, Son, and Holy Ghost.'

'A nice idea!' His voice sounded unconvinced.

'Are you being ironic?'

'No', he replied with more than a hint of guilt.

'You should be careful not to offend our deities. Mokosh, the goddess of destiny, may be a lovely young woman who spins the thread of life, but she is also dangerous. Sometimes we Slavs call her Srecha.' Then she began to recite:

> Where Alatyr, 'father of stones', is;
> On that stone Altyr
> On her throne
> Sits the maiden king.
> Mistress of needlework,
> She passes her golden thread
> Through [the eye of] a steel needle
> And sews up bloody wounds

Tom sat in silent awe for a moment, braced by the heartfelt veracity of her words. Ekaterina's hair cascaded over her shoulders, her pointing breasts staring down at him. She had the shapely hips and slender legs of her horseback ancestors. He could easily imagine her thundering across the windswept steppes, loosing arrows at Mongol raiders, riding her steed hard into the ripped, red heart of a stormy sunset.

They opened some wine. Ekaterina kicked off her shoes and unzipped her jeans. 'I think I'm getting drunk', she said, fingers loosening his tie. He saw she wore the mask of a Veely water sprite dancing and singing in the mountain springs. Tom pushed her back onto the bed, thumbs slipping under her briefs and sliding thin cotton down over her knees.

❖ Celtic Cross flags begin appearing on prominent buildings and national monuments across Russia;

❖ Mass rallies are held in Perm's Gorkovo Park and along Lenina and Komsomolsky Prospekt. 'We demand our city stays Russian' echoes across the Kama River;

❖ Slavic Force and Russian Action militants seize the Kremlin government building of Nizhny Novgorod and arrest the Supreme Regional Officer;

❖ Army Brigades rally volunteers in city and town squares, distributing food and munitions, as well as providing basic arms training;

❖ Right and Left gangs clash across the country;

❖ The military imposes local curfews to prevent looting and disorder.

The wind came biting off the Baltic. Frost-hard teeth raked flesh. Tom cut a thin, black figure on the bleak expanse of the Dvortsovvy Most as Arkady approached, wearing a long greatcoat, his bulky body acting as a windbreaker.

'*Privet!*' he declared as he came close. 'You are tired, no?'

'*Nyet*', the Professor replied.

'You look like you burn candle at both ends!'

Tom shrugged. 'I am still celebrating our success!'

'Or maybe you can't handle our girls?' Arkady laughed.

'I told you to leave her out of this!'

'You don't tell me, shit!'

'But burning the apartment?'

'You were warned!'

'But that is ridiculous. A speech . . .'

Arkady cut him off. 'Is incendiary!'

'It makes no sense . . .' Arkady's fist hit him square on the nose. Tom saw a spark of light in the back of his brain and felt hot blood spurt down his shirt. He attempted to stay on his feet, but a second swinging blow to the temple sent him staggering back against the bridge railings. He stared at the ground, trying to focus, stammering his words until Arkady took him firmly by the arm and flagged down the car he had used to chase Tom and Ekaterina down Nevsky Prospekt.

'Get in!' Arkady shouted, pushing Tom onto the backseat. 'It is too cold to stand outside debating', he said, slamming the door, signalling Bogdan to move on. All the familiar streets rushed by the windows. Arkady handed Tom a handkerchief. 'Clean yourself!' he ordered, 'I don't want you to bleed all over the upholstery.'

'The girl's got nothing to do with this . . .'

'She's one of you!'

'No!'

'Don't lie!'

'I'm not.' Tom spat a loose tooth.

'We know she attends street speeches by fascists.'

'She's just an impressionable student.'

'Then you people should not be giving dangerous lectures, yes?'

'I'll leave if you agree not to harm her.'

'This is a civil war, you think we care about whether you stay or go?'

'You firebomb old men!'

'And Blood and Honour stabs our boys!'

'I don't advocate violence!'

'You are complicit!' The car swept up to the kerbside outside the Astoria. Arkady brandished a Stechkin pistol fitted with a long silencer before the Englishman's eyes. 'You have 24 hours to leave, after that, this goes pop and your body goes swim in the Neva, understand?' Then he pulled open the door and bundled Tom into the gutter. 'And I'll fuck your pretty friend just for fun', he smirked, as the car drove off into slow, swirling traffic.

When he got to his room, Ekaterina was gone. A handwritten note said, 'I have an idea!' Tom stripped and ran a shower. As he stepped into the surging water, the phone began to ring. He ignored it, washing away humiliating memories with soap and bath oils. Later, he swallowed aspirin with a slug of Jack Daniels and massaged his creaking jaw. Arkady's attack had been so quick, the blows so accurate. He thought of the power of the disorientating strike on the side of his head and the ease with which he had been thrown around. No simple heavy could have handled him with such confidence. He had been served notice.

Meanwhile, Ekaterina's idea, communicated in garbled fashion via mobile to Alexei and Yuri's Vulcari, involved a surprise attack on Arkady's base in Ulitsa Egorova. They were joined by Roman, Tom's taxi transfer from Pulkovo airport, and their new recruit, Saniya. Ill-timed and ill-equipped, they had rushed into action without waiting for Alyosha, or their new mentor, Peter Janssen. Bald Bogdan was the first to hear them coming. He went silent, waving a large hand, signalling the others to be quiet before picking up his SR-2 and rising from the armchair.

Unclipping the safety, Arkady, still nursing grazed knuckles, had drawn the Stechkin from his shoulder holster. Moving to the door, his head gestured for his sidekick to respond to Yuri's demanding knock and unconvincing claim that he had a package to deliver. Others were reaching for the AO-63 assault rifles piled against the wall. Barrels were soon pointing, ammo clips strapped together with insulation tape.

When Bogdan's hand swung the door open, Alexei and Yuri led the knife-wielding charge straight at the guns. The first volley punched holes through their faces, serrating arms and legs, body parts spliced clean off the bone. Saniya's intestines spiralled like pork sausage onto the carpet.

9.

The future truly is ours.—Alexander Dugin

They stood with crowds of young nationalists amidst a sea of banners in front of the city's eternal flame, commemorating the lives of French partisans Sabine D'Orlac and Luc Dubois, whose deaths had just been announced on Russia Today. People held cold hands to the rippling red tongues rising out of the charred earth before them, passing beer bottles, strumming guitars.

'We come here a lot', Ekaterina was saying as a friend rolled what appeared to be a concoction of Russian and Lebanese blends, wrapped loosely in flapping cigarette papers. 'It all started with Borovikov's death in 2006, but now we know we have to do more than just protest.' Some students stood, hands on hips, singing forlornly at the Moon, thin bodies weaving shadows in the firelight, hypnotic voices trailing off into frosty starlight. Tom recognised the chords of Ian Stuart's 'Gone with the Breeze' and the familiar lyric being pronounced with a Russian accent.

Tom was surprised to see Vladimir, Ekaterina's would-be suitor, mount the wall, blonde quiff waving in the wind. His slender figure wrapped in a black leather jacket, he cut a dashing figure in the moonshine. 'Comrades', he bawled over an ocean of pale faces. 'I say it is time to serve justice on the mobsters that have robbed us every day of our lives, our parents' lives, and our grandparents' lives! They controlled our money, invited invaders to take our women, and they spat on our dignity. I say the counter-revolution has begun. It is time to take back what is ours and hang the bastards by the neck. *Rossiiya! Rossiiya! Rossiiya!*'

'Vlad is one who yearns for martyrdom', Ekaterina confirmed. 'The example of Luc and Sabine will be strong with him forever.' Then, after standing in a minute's silent tribute as the scissor breeze rolled in off the Neva, army trucks pulled up and began handing out weapons to the young revolutionaries.

Tom watched his partner take a matte-black OTs-33 as they stood under the crisping tree branches, her hair silvering with hoarfrost, snowflakes settling on the dome of the Church on the Spilled Blood, looming broodily over the Moika. Tom squeezed her empty hand, but Ekaterina's eyes were fixed on the machine pistol and its 27-round magazine, red lips folded in defiance.

'Katja?'

She turned to him, the glow of the eternal flame preserved in her retina.

'Another time of troubles', she said, leading him towards the embankment where stone melted away into the icy water. Cars were moving at top speed, ignoring the falling sleet, heading in the direction of the Hermitage, towards the bridges over to the islands.

Tom felt he was wading through shallow water, giddy roofscapes distorted by winter light, merging apartments and government buildings. 'Do you know', she said, '200,000 White émigrés left Russia during the Revolution? Many of our greatest philosophers, historians, and professors were exiled from here, forced aboard a German ship called the *Oberbürgermeister Haken* at the Naberezhnaya Leitenanta Shmidta.'

'Not killed?'

'Lenin didn't kill everyone', she grinned. 'Stalin, on the other hand!'

'Where did they go?'

'Berlin, Prague, Paris . . . all the usual places.'

❖ The Karaganov Doctrine of protecting Russian ethnic populations wherever they may be is enacted;

❖ Despite objections from the UN, Russia restarts its humanitarian aid for those refugees living in Donbass;

❖ Alexander Dugin returns from exile;
❖ Naval patrols on the Volga bombard Muslim settlements;
❖ Russia moves 50,000 troops and fighter aircraft to Sumy, close to the Ukrainian border;
❖ Spetsnaz operatives fight hand-to-hand with Mujahideen forces and Pakistani special services in Ust-Labinsk;
❖ Russia withdraws its nuclear and strategic capability to within its newly defined ethno-state borders, defended along the line of the Pechora and Ural rivers in the north and east and the Volga in the west.

After making love, they fell asleep in each other's arms. An hour or so after midnight, Tom woke to find her missing. He wrapped himself in a towel and went into the lounge. Ekaterina was turned towards the window, her head in her hands.

'I sent them there', she was saying. 'I am responsible.' Tom stared at her long, straight back, salt tears running through the cracks in her fingers. She waited a few minutes before turning to look at him. 'And my grandfather, too?' A question mark hung like a huge wire coat hanger off her lower lip.

'That was not you. They did that to get at me.'

'Then it is both of us!'

'Yes', he had to admit. 'It is both of us.'

'You know', she said, 'in 1945, a famous Russian poet fell in love with a professor from Oxford University who visited her one cold November night, and stayed talking with her until the dawn.' Tom hunched his shoulders. 'She called him her "Guest from the future" . . .'

'Were they happy together?'

'No, he returned to his dreaming spires, and the Soviets withdrew the writer's state privileges and banned her poetry.'

There was a long silence as they both looked at the

loaded gun on the table. 'And just like him, you will leave?' she said, almost accusingly. He felt intimidated. 'It is said the poet used to stand by the window, waiting for him to return.'

Tom was in front of a firing squad. He moved forward, sweeping her up in his arms, holding her so close that his lonely heart could feel hers beat against his chest.

'I won't let you down', he promised, knowing that he would.

'Kiss me, you bastard!' she whispered with that deep, throaty English, barely passing for European, but offering salvation for the West.

Peter Janssen was exasperated by news of the loss of the Vulcari cell. Tossing his trilby on to the bed, he cursed Yuri and Alexei, but having met Ekaterina in the doorway to his apartment block earlier, he fully realised how events had played out. Janssen had already spoken to Alyosha and Grigori, and decided on a course of action. There was no turning back. He moved over to the wardrobe and pulled out a tan leather briefcase, easing the well-oiled zip the full length of the binding so as to lift the lid. Inside was a Tec-9 'spray and pay' machine pistol. Janssen assembled the weapon, twisting on the long graphite sound suppressor with a scratchy, metallic grimace.

Outside, there was a hint of moonglow across the frosted rooftops looking out over the river. Some cloud cover offered the potential for surprise, mostly by smothering the stars to the north with polluted petroleum fumes. Janssen advanced thoughtfully, combing the Nevsky for a taxi ride, wild cats rummaging through garbage, stopping for a moment to scan him with feline eyes that gleamed in car headlights before fading as the motor moved on. It was cold, too cold for love, but just right for killing.

Two Bloc heavies wearing woollen hats pulled down to their eyebrows hovered in the foyer at Ulitsa Egorova. One sat back on a chair, hands in pockets, legs stretched out, ankles crossed, causing his boots to form a V pattern on the uneven tiles. The other was leaning against the wall, slitted eyes flitting all over the hallway. The man in the chair shifted position as a European in a triby and long, black coat entered from off the road, jerking his head lazily at his Tartar companion, who managed an incoherent grunt before pushing himself away from the wall.

'Can I help you?' he asked in monosyllabic Russian to a man who spoke no Russian beyond, '*Da Tovarich, och-en-pree-yat-na?*' The muzzle flash from Janssen's gun punctured the guard's forehead like a hammer on a nail. The guy on the chair tried to wrestle an MP-446 pistol out of the folds of his jacket. The executioner stepped forward, kicking his jaw and sending him flying backwards, chair sliding, the man toppling, Janssen finishing him with one bullet square to the back of his head.

Stepping around jetting blood, Peter pushed the button in front of him. The lift rose slowly to the floor where Janssen knew Arkady and Bogdan to be hiding. The ping of the elevator's arrival echoed in the corridor. As the doors slid open, Janssen stepped out just in time to meet a Bloc member coming to check who was there. The Antifa man's face fell open as the first bullet took off his testicles and the second burst his Adam's apple like a failed William Tell re-enactment.

Heaving the corpse aside, Janssen shouldered his way through the door frame, subliminally clocking the chipped woodwork where his protégés had met their end. '*Dobre Vechyre*', he announced to the assembled crowd before easing the Tec-9 into auto and letting off like a threshing machine. Two died instantly. A third, Bogdan, collapsed with a leg wound, whimpering and begging for mercy.

Arkady's huge body slid across the wooden table, his Stechkin blowing mouse holes in the ceiling. Janssen grinned, inserting a second magazine. He enjoyed killing with impunity. Striding over to where the bald Bloc fanatic lay clutching his shattered knee-cap, he placed the gun barrel to Bogdan's juddering skull. His opponent's tears

Fenek Solère

flowed freely, Then he tugged at the trigger triumphantly.

10.

In Petersburg I am a tourist, an observer, not an inhabitant.—Andrei Bely

Tom walked alone in the heart of the city. Moonlight played on granite. He was caught up in a world-changing event. His eyes darted wildly from the mosque burning in the distance to the Bakhcha-U parked at the side of the road. It was becoming increasingly obvious that he was a man of letters, not action, his world inhabited by characters like Stavrogin and Verkhovensky, Dostoevsky's political villains, rather than the muscle-bound reality of Bogdan and Arkady. The vision of Ekaterina lying asleep and the metallic click of the door latch dropping made his conscience itch.

He strode on, not knowing or caring where. He circled the canal bridges, lost in thought, up and down, past the Anichkovsky Palace and the sleek horse statues harnessed by straps of bitter starlight. Strings of white globes stretched away down Nevsky, their light casting neon nets over the muddy water flowing to the sea. Carved gargoyles looked down accusingly. Tom kept asking himself what he should do. Should he stay or should he go? He was sweating despite the cold. The ghoulish grandeur rolled out either side of the river before him. Corruption and glamour were covered by a twinkle of silver. He remembered she had told him that in the Russian language, St Petersburg is male whilst Moscow is female. Little sentences and sayings, the sound of her voice reverberated constantly in his head. He leaned against a parapet, steadying himself against the maelstrom loosed about him.

The city was in a hurry. It was as if the residents were recovering from collective amnesia. Granules of snow flit-

tered through car headlights, ice crunched like baby pow-
der underfoot. He knew he had to get back to the hotel.
He was so tired that he began to stagger. His moleskin
coat was speckled with flakes, and kiss-curls were stuck to
his forehead. The lines from Dugin's alias Hans Zivers
came to mind: 'In a buttoned coat, buttoned frock coat,
solemnly kefir he drinks, and the dogs bark, and move
black cancers, in the darkness of Soviet apartments'.

- ❖ Her Majesty's Consulate in St Petersburg advises all
  British citizens to leave Russia as a consequence of
  the deteriorating political situation;
- ❖ Russian nationalists re-capture the radar base at
  Gabala and launch sporadic attacks amidst the
  rusting derricks dotted along the Caspian shore,
  shelling the Bibi Heyat mosque and the new fortress housing Israel's Kohanim Council of the East;
- ❖ 'Our new challenge', states General Hosiah Webb,
  Commander of the US 4th Army in Afghanistan, 'is
  to secure the energy corridor between the Caspian
  and the Balkans, those like Baku–Tbilisi–Ceyhan
  and Nabucco, supplying our allies in Western Europe';
- ❖ Petro Poroshenko demands direct military intervention to save Jews from persecution in Russia;
- ❖ Wall Street financial houses redouble their efforts
  to undermine the rouble by hiking interest rates
  yet again;
- ❖ Firms trading in global equity markets start a frenzy of selling on what they deem to be contaminat-
  ed funds on the instruction of the Zew Research
  Group based in Strasbourg, New York, and Tel
  Aviv;
- ❖ Food processing plants in Belarus are sabotaged by
  NATO special forces.

Tom's eyes reluctantly welcomed the first rays of dawn
light playing like pellucid fingers over the bedsheets. He

lay still for a minute, his head on the soft pillow, his penis hard as rock. He had been dreaming of a woman walking through cornfields, tresses flowing from a crown of spring flowers, bearing an apple in open hands.

'Where am I?' he said to himself. 'What have I done?'

He got up to use the toilet and saw the brown suitcase in the hall. Then he remembered everything. The League's request for him to attend an emergency council. His promise. Her smiling through tears and Arkady's threat. Could he stay and fight? Could he cut and run?

Tom fell heavily onto the toilet seat. His sweaty face reflected in the mirror between the chrome taps. He could already hear the sound of cracking bones and see his blood smeared on a wall. He was not going to die here like Yesenin. Poets die romantically, but political dissidents like him bleed painfully in shootouts with the police, like that young French duo in Arles. Neither did he care to end his days like that Trotsky acolyte John Reed, author of the book he had just cast into the wastepaper basket, squirming in agony on a hospital bed with spotted typhus.

He swallowed some aspirin and took a long swig from a bottle. His eyes were sore. He could not be sure if it was from the drink or the tears he remembered coming suddenly in the early hours.

His hand reached for the phone. 'I need a taxi', he heard himself say, and then in response to the voice on the other end, 'To the airport.' He got dressed, brushed his hair, and checked his wallet. Picking up his bags, he walked out the door without looking back. Behind him, the phone began to ring.

Downstairs, the lobby was full of cleaners pushing mops and empty-handed doormen looking for something to do. Life went on. One anaemic youngster with bad skin offered to take his luggage. Tom waved him away, then gestured to the girl at the desk, who in turn pointed to a black-suited driver walking towards him across the foamy floor.

'Oh, excuse me, sir, but I have a letter for you', the re-

ceptionist remembered, coming out from behind the
counter to hand him a sealed envelope. Tom took it, but
before he could peel it open, his driver was guiding his
arm.

'Your car, sir!' Tom pushed the blue envelope into his
coat pocket and followed the chauffeur out onto the
street. A gypsy woman was passing, carrying a sprig of
flowers.

'Would you like to buy one for your sweetheart?' she
asked in broken English. Tom chose some, paid her, and
tossed it onto the back seat. The driver slammed the trunk
on his baggage.

'*Pulkovo, spasibo*', the Englishman said. The engine
started and they pulled off into the square.

He looked up at St Isaacs as they circled, watching a
young family walking their brown water spaniel under the
sparse trees. Peter Janssen was strolling, bag in hand, towards the Astoria. Alyosha was at his side. A column of
armed Vulcari trailed in their wake. They went over the
Blue Bridge and up Voznesenkiy Prospect. Glass shop
fronts winked with cracked smiles. They stopped only to
cut right back across the Fontanka embankment to make
Moskovskiy Prospekt, then went onwards past the Technology Institute and the Olympic Gardens. For a moment,
his attention was drawn once again to the ubiquitous Lenin statue, this time pointing towards the airport. Iron railings rushed past. He could see the dusty towers of the Baltic railway station in the distance and endless rows of Stalinist housing blocks. Alex Tiuniaev's heart-rending sym-
phony *I Knew Her* played on the radio.

30 minutes and 5 checkpoints later, the car pulled up at
Pulkovo. 'Take the flowers to this address.' He handed the
driver a hastily scribbled note. 'It is very important that
you do not say where I am, *horosho?*' Tom turned up his
collar and walked across the tarmac between two Chosta
self-propelled howitzers which were entering the depar-
ture terminal. Passing security, he set off a metal detector
and had to empty his pockets, allowing the hands of a

stripling security guard to run over his body. Two pin-sharp eyes stared him out. Tom returned the look with interest, regretting his insolence when he was pulled un-ceremoniously aside.

'Papers, please?' A flat, outstretched hand commanded an instant response. When he saw the British passport, the Slav's face split open. 'James Bond, right?'

'Yeah, 007!'

The young man slapped his shoulder with genuine warmth, then continued, stumbling over his words, 'Null, null sem, your mission is over, God save the Queen!' Tom laughed, pocketing his passport and moving away, anx-ious not to draw any further attention to himself. His flight was still hours away, so he took the escalator up to the first floor. There were a few newsstands and gift shops still operating along the mezzanine. A husband and wife bought a map of London marked with Cyrillic script. The couple were pointing out Big Ben and the London Eye to their kids. It was obvious they were the first of many refu-gees anticipating Armageddon, pretending to leave for a short vacation, but in reality planning never to return. He recognised the words 'Madame Tussauds' and went off to buy a coffee.

Tom took an empty table and sat alone, wondering if flights would be cancelled or if he would be stopped from boarding. He was not taking the calls or texts that Grigori was sending every 10 minutes. The coffee tasted like river silt. He drank it anyway, grains and all. It was something to do. People moved around him, talking, shouting, smok-ing cigarettes. There was an endless babble of excitement and confusion about the unfolding situation. The travel-lers' eyes were drawn to the black electronic screens with rolling green lettering, telling them when they could board their flights. Helsinki, Oslo, and Milan came up ear-ly. A hijack in Kaliningrad meant the outbound to London was delayed. His anxiety began to mount. He sat staring down the clock, willing time to disappear. Eventually, they announced his flight, and he moved through passport

control, first heading for a bar where three Mediterrane-
an-looking girls were parked uncomfortably on stools before using a hand basin in the restroom to freshen his face.
The obligatory duty free shop was not especially inspiring.
He hovered for a little while over the perfumes and linge-
rie, wondering who to buy them for. There was no one
left. No one at home.

Around 17.00, he stepped onto the escalator to the de-
parture gate, queueing for the final security check, shuffling off his shoes, getting frisked once again. His fellow
passengers were already passing through the sliding doors
to the West. For a moment, the Englishman hesitated, still
pondering his options. A stewardess asked for his boarding card. Her eyes flitted over the incomprehensible markings. A red nail pointed him in the direction of the air-
plane.

Once aboard, he threw his jacket into the overhead
compartment, and the blue envelope handed to him by
the hotel receptionist floated down into the aisle. Picking
it up, he took his seat by the window. Engines cranked
into operation and roared as they powered the plane along
the runway, lifting the undercarriage. Then there was that
sudden, gut-churning moment when they left the ground.
The plane banked to the west, flying out over the Gulf of
Finland. From his seat, Tom watched as a cold winter Sun
burst through the misty sky, shooting dirty clouds with
rocket fire. To the east, frozen rain crystals sparkled like
wet diamonds showering down over the city's fading skyline. He could just make out St Isaac's golden dome and
the smoking factory towers shrinking as they climbed.

The Professor removed his glasses, pinching the bridge
of his nose. Swallowing hard, his fingers nervously handled the letter. He smelled it and recognised the delicate
handwriting. It was dated for that day. Sliding the white
sheet out, he read:

> . . . absence is the best medicine
> for forgetting . . . but the best way

to forget forever is to see daily . . .
—Anna Akhmatova

Below him, he could see the rugged land turn to frozen sea. Black cranes lurched drunkenly on the derelict docks, warehouses falling off the shore. A criss-cross of clear blue sword-slashes ran between endless plates of ice. Their pure, flat surfaces scraped by the wind, forming a stiff, white crust over the Baltic. Every now and then, a rusting red ship would cut a channel through the sheets en route to Denmark, Sweden, or Norway. He imagined some seasoned captain at their helm, steering cargo westwards, guided as much by his nose as the 1950s navigation equipment that bleeped on the oil-splattered screen in his cabin. There he stood, the pilot, riding the waves, pushing on through the gulf towards a point where the sea met the sky in a rapture of crushed turquoise.

Further out at sea, the sky became thick and overcast. Tom's gaze followed the plane's wingtip as it passed over one small island after another, until at last these isolated rock outcrops, stretching toward Scandinavia, were swallowed by the crash of hungry waves. The aircraft pierced the mocha meniscus of the cloud line. Engines accelerated at full throttle. With the jet's roar throbbing in his ears, he twisted his neck one last time to see the lights of St Petersburg slowly disappear in a warm glow over the eastern horizon. Leaning back in his seat, he felt thankful to have been present at the birth of Russia's new revolution. 'And now to liberate the West', he swore to himself.

Konets

ABOUT THE AUTHOR

Fenek Solère writes novels in the tradition of the New Right. Following his critically acclaimed debut novel *The Partisan* (2014), he has published articles at Counter-Currents/*North American New Right* and the *New European Conservative* websites and has been interviewed at *Radix.*

www.ingramcontent.com/pod-product-compliance
Lightning Source LLC
Chambersburg PA
CBHW051300250626
47155CB00009B/3364